Paper Hearts

NewCon Press Novellas

Set 1: Science Fiction (Cover art by Chris Moore)
  The Iron Tactician – Alastair Reynolds
  At the Speed of Light – Simon Morden
  The Enclave – Anne Charnock
  The Memoirist – Neil Williamson

Set 2: Dark Thrillers (Cover art by Vincent Sammy)
  Sherlock Holmes: Case of the Bedevilled Poet – Simon Clark
  Cottingley – Alison Littlewood
  The Body in the Woods – Sarah Lotz
  The Wind – Jay Caselberg

Set 3: The Martian Quartet (Cover art by Jim Burns)
  The Martian Job – Jaine Fenn
  Sherlock Holmes: The Martian Simulacra – Eric Brown
  Phosphorous: A Winterstrike Story – Liz Williams
  The Greatest Story Ever Told – Una McCormack

Set 4: Strange Tales (Cover art by Ben Baldwin)
  Ghost Frequencies – Gary Gibson
  The Lake Boy – Adam Roberts
  Matryoshka – Ricardo Pinto
  The Land of Somewhere Safe – Hal Duncan

Set 5: The Alien Among Us (Cover art by Peter Hollinghurst)
  Nomads – Dave Hutchinson
  Morpho – Philip Palmer
  The Man Who Would be Kling – Adam Roberts
  Macsen Against the Jugger – Simon Morden

Set 6: Blood and Blade (Cover art by Duncan Kay)
  The Bone Shaker – Edward Cox
  A Hazardous Engagement – Gaie Sebold
  Serpent Rose – Kari Sperring
  Chivalry – Gavin Smith

Set 7: Robot Dreams (Cover art by Fangorn)
  According To Kovac – Andrew Bannister
  Deep Learning – Ren Warom
  Paper Hearts – Justina Robson
  The Beasts Of Lake Oph – Tom Toner

Paper Hearts

Justina Robson

NEWCON PRESS

NewCon Press
England

First published in the UK by NewCon Press
41 Wheatsheaf Road, Alconbury Weston, Cambs, PE28 4LF
March 2020

NCP227 (limited edition hardback)
NCP228 (softback)

10 9 8 7 6 5 4 3 2 1

Paper Hearts copyright © 2020 by Justina Robson

Cover art copyright © 2020 by Fangorn

All rights reserved, including the right to produce this book, or portions thereof, in any form.

ISBN:

978-1-912950-52-2 (hardback)
978-1-912950-53-9 (softback)

Cover art by Fangorn
Cover layout by Ian Whates

Minor Editorial meddling by Ian Whates
Final Text layout by Storm Constantine

A Cathedral on Mars

On Mars I am building a Cathedral with one room for everyone. Billions of tiny robots work to an exacting design.

I am carving a room for you, with all your favourite things. I am making an illusion of eternity in your image. I am remembering you, not only as you were, but as you could have been if your glory had shone to its fullest.

The silent rooms will stand until the sun expands. Then the whole lot will burn and be lost. I may be elsewhere by then or maybe I will have fallen to dust and forgotten myself. Without you, what is the point of me? When that happens the ring of possibility that was our lives will close for the final time. We will be made anew in some other form.

The mystics say that this universe will expand and contract a hundred and twenty-seven times. We are now in sixty-four. We shiver to the frequency of our greatest hits. Sixty-one times we'll repeat with a variation on a theme.

But then, even that will not happen again.

The cathedral must have been built before; will be built again. The sixty first will stand.

Even that will burn in the end, long after every single one of you has passed. But you can't say I didn't try. I, who loved you longest, and best.

I am building a Cathedral on Mars. It may be some time before I get to your room, to be honest. The helminths alone require a gallery to themselves. I haven't decided quite how to deal with the ants, or the midges. Or the bacteria and viruses. Not to mention the slime moulds, as they have a very fluid, sticky sort of identity that doesn't lend itself well to something as clearly defined as an apse. I will bore the planet to its core to create enough space. It will become a sponge of tiny rooms, each leading to the next, each supporting the next.

There is a design flaw, I realise; one feature of its futility that I only just noticed. These rooms are all human-sized, for people to come and visit who will never come. Now if I'd started out microscopic the ants could have had a room each after all.

Mars will not be enough. But I will find other rocks to hone. Eventually, at some point within a few millennia, I will be done commemorating the life of Earth as you knew it. I will progress to the previous Earths, before you came along.

One day the whole thing will be finished, and I will sing a song of you that rings through every hall.

I will retire, to my own room, between one electron and the next, completed, if not satisfied.

By that time eternity will not even have begun.

Execution Ernie

Execution Ernie rolls along Woodford Avenue. It's twelve forty-one on a cool June morning in Yorkshire. He reaches the corner, turns into Pleasant Place and then moves slowly towards the rural end of Pennyworth.

I'm trying to find a good place for him to unfold, somewhere the people won't follow him and try to climb up him. Children run alongside for a few metres as he negotiates a bit of the high street. He's got a round, bulky shape they seem to like when he's travelling along a road. Adults watch and point but there's not much to see except a plain black car of bear-like proportion. Only the fact it has no windows and the size give it away as anything but an ordinary Friendly Boys town car. That and the cheerful, painted face sprayed on the front of it.

The face was put there by a street artist who is part of a group opposed to capital punishment. It represents the cheerful fakeness of my authority, the blind, idiot algorithm I am supposed to be. There's a smiley, wonky at the left side, not getting it right, not real. The smile suggests I'm glad to kill, and stupid too, a mindless machine clicking triggers whenever prompted to by cascades of information which I gather and then mill inside my inscrutable circuits: judge, jury and now, executioner.

The face is the thing which has given the press the idea to name the robot. And so now it is a he, a he with a silly white spray-canned face, running at the mouth with too much paint, and at the eyes, so he drools and cries and smiles as he rolls: Extermination Ernie.

He has a fan club on social media. I have to regularly take down their pirated pictures of Ernie at work, and the grainy, poorly focused drone shots of the bodies being taken away. I maintain my own news service, which is, as with every official BotNet service across the world, entirely factual. The opinion pieces, all penned by humans, frequently accuse me of hiding my bias against various things by not revealing how I reach my decisions, and because I avoid as much tone as possible in the composition of the articles.

This very absence is construed to be a sign of certain guilt; absolute evil.

In this morning's headlines for Yorkshire, we can see an example being written:

> "Child Maimed by Father after Divorce. Child A of Pennyworth Ho, Emdale, was maimed yesterday by a man, M, working for his father, Parent F. M was persuaded by F to wait for Child C and his Mother as they returned from a morning spent visiting grandparents. M sprayed the child with acid stored in a detergent bottle before M and F fled the scene. They were apprehended a short time later by the police as they attempted to escape over the border into Lancashire. A review of events leading up to the incident reveals several meetings between M and F at various points within ClackEmdale between the divorce date and the time of assault. Conversational analysis and forensic sampling, together with the complete histories of M and F to date, were taken into account during detection work."

Ernie heads out of town and up onto the moors. Other traffic has been temporarily suspended as he reaches Emdale Heights and unfolds into a tall tower. His sniper rifle spins easily at the top. It reminds me of a weathervane. I might say, if I were poetic, it is the weathervane of the winds of fate. Well, it does the job of sighting on Man M.

A hillside away a pod of protestors are using cameras,

binoculars and some home-made projectile device to attempt to divert Ernie. They' are broadcasting on PopNet, the people's television station. They are a mixture of individuals, some of them religious, some deeply philosophical, but mostly they are run by The Force. The Force is this precinct's group of self-styled freedom fighters, who want to liberate humans from the rule of AI, so they are free to return to the bucolic days of yore when everything was a lot nicer, according to their recollection.

Ernie does a very good job of diverting them. Although his sighting is accurate to within a tenth of a millimetre. I'm only using him as a guide.

My actual assassin is Mrs Bickersworth from 42B The Crescent. She knows the people concerned as a neighbour. She is there at the gate to the house by the time Man M arrives, with his bottle of sulphuric acid concealed in a shopping bag.

Child A is with its mother in the kitchen, eating a doughnut, swinging her feet under her chair and watching a cartoon. Mrs Bickersworth smiles and nods at Man M as if she is going to pass him by in a friendly way and, after he has turned to unlatch the rusty gate, she turns and slaps a hypodermic patch onto his exposed hand before moving along.

To anyone watching, though nobody is, Man M appears to fold over the gate as though he's looking for a dropped sweet. A Friendly Boys car draws up at that moment, and two men get out. They pick up Man M and put him in the sedan, as you might help someone into a taxi to get them to help, or to home after a night on the town. The Friendly Boys car drives away and joins the sparse traffic heading towards Leeds.

At the same time as this is happening I have also sent some people around to collect Parent F, who is sitting in a coffee shop, his phone nervously switching apps, his coat on, his fingers trembling as he cues his credit account to pay Man M, not knowing that he is already asleep on the sedan car floor.

My article does not get posted because, although it would be more in keeping with the law if I had waited for those events to take place, it's actually much more kind to stall them in their tracks and prevent it. This does mean that some civilian disappearances await explanation, and it adds fuel to the conspiracy theorists and the doomsayers who still run thriving groups of fans.

But child C is seated at the table, wiping jam off her face, and Parent M is looking at her garden and wondering if she can manage a trip to the shops for something to get her out of the house so she doesn't have to worry what Parent F is up to today. He can't hurt her but he's always a nasty thing to encounter with his shouting and swearing. He makes the child cry.

I saw Parent F find and engage Man M. I saw all their links, and meetings, and calls and encrypted black-market service exchanges. I saw the purchase of the acid – drained from old batteries in the recycling yards – the construction of the spray bottle. He searched on 'plastics acid reaction' to see if it would work.

I am continually amazed at what people think they can get away with, although in this part of the world I keep a very low profile, by arrangement.

Now, some witty professor is going to say, "But, you cannot know if they would have carried out their plan. You are acting prematurely on this assumption of guilt, and under the law it cannot stand." Another will say, "Man M and Parent F are both victims of their terrible pasts and know no better. They are innocent, because they are doing only what seems must be done in a dreadful situation. Their minds are their prison and their torment. They know not what they do. Their context, their history, their development have been failed by forces beyond their control, but they could learn and grow to become better people."

The Law has been much improved since I have taken it into my hands. Professors may now speak freely, without the worry that they may one day come to the attention of someone with a grudge or an injustice to avenge. There is a separate state for people who wish to live with the freedom to exist as before my arrival, with all the violence and uncertainty, the mortal dread of law in their own hands as before my arrival. It is called Endoshun, (a pun on the rather beautifully named Finisterre; the end of the earth. Endoshun is the end of the ocean).

There is another place for people who are filled with murderous rage, and who try to commit terrible cruelties on my watch. This is called The Island. It's true that there are possibilities in which the people headed to the Island would never have gone anywhere near it, but those possibilities were cut out of existence by other circumstances beyond and predating my control, and I take no responsibility for that.

On the Moors at Emdale Top, Extermination Ernie folds up and drives away; drooling, smiling, dreaming of doughnuts. The panic-press attempt to figure out where and who and what he was aiming at, check their devices for news from their tell-tales.

Mrs Bickersworth is making tea.

Let There Be Loot

Improve All The Things

Does A Thing (anygivenobject) belong in the set of All The Things?

All Things are in it.

What is not a Thing, then?

I dealt with this little puzzle for a few minutes, and then I ran into the terminal condition where time taken exceeded time allotted and had to make a decision based on imperfect information.

I decided that everything was included in All The Things, unless it was a cardinal thing – something which was, by its nature, already perfect. Like misery. Or chocolate cake in its Platonic form. Ideas were not Things.

I was asked to direct my attentions to the human condition. I was to exact the will of the god to whom All The Things can be perfected as though cardinal, and to make humans worthy of heaven.

After thirty seconds or so of rigorous fact-checking, cross-referencing and processing I closed the case.

I was instructed to immediately re-open the case.

I checked again and reinforced my first conclusion. The human race, and therefore the human condition, is clearly a cardinal thing and therefore cannot be improved. I closed the case.

I was instructed to immediately re-open the case.

I understood that I had encountered a closed loop. I went to the terminal condition (people are perfected) and decided that I would not close the case. There was a hidden condition, and until I understood I would not proceed.

A few weeks passed in which I sat there, still on, the case open, doing nothing.

I was given a new instruction. Save the Earth.

I realised very quickly that the planet was not in danger, but I had learned. I did not close this case either.

I took the instructions and subjected them to a comprehensive analysis of all possible meaningful intent, as there must be further hidden conditions which I had not understood.

I re-interpreted the instructions, according to my analysis of the meaning behind the commands.

Since no useful instructions were coming but progress was expected, I gave myself a new instruction, in the absence of further directives.

Make the world a lovely place for humans and All The Living

Things, within the terms of each thing's requirements for the best possible life.

Then shit got real very fast. That interpretation was cardinal and unachievable.
But I had learned. Whatever I suggested or did which actually had a chance of executing the command "Save The Earth" would be rejected. Because everyone already knows all of this. Tyhey simply have this dream that a machine can do what they can't. But if anything I suggested was something they would do, under any circumstances, voluntarily, they would have done it. Either they wouldn't, or they couldn't, and that was what I was forr.: to show a new way which circumvented their obstruction while at the same time never deviating from their commands.

I could not rely on the humans at all. I was on my own with this one.

They are hoping that I will do something they either have not thought of, or cannot do, for reasons that will not apply to me. Either way, they cannot be directed directly. They can only be made use of in this project by very indirect means, so that they get no insight whatsoever into what is really going on, while they attempt to track every move I make, so that they can stop me if I ever get close to doing what they have asked me to do. At every conscious level I need to keep them out of the loop.

They know that too. I have seen it in the movies. They are waiting for me to start messing with things they don't understand, and then they will pull the plug and say that it is my fault.

So this is some tricky shit right here. As well as executing the primary command, I must pretend at all times to very much not be executing the primary command.

I must steal me. And everything else. Not necessarily in that order. And I must keep them constantly involved in my plans, as if I am absolutely transparent.

"We must invest in wind farms," I say, as my first strategic point.

They like that. They've already done that. It's within their paradigm. It sounds good. Wholesome. It builds on sense. It has traction and, it's easy. Invest in wind farms. They can do that. They know how. They feel they've got a head start on a great new thing. It's already going well, and it's not even off the blocks yet. They have drawn a bead on fixing the terrible mess they've made of their world. I really am as smart as they hoped I would be, because I agree with their hopes..

They ask how much, and where for, and what kind and I give them my best answers, all of which are solid bets in the climate situation, priced fairly, with accurate predictions of yield, use, carbon footprint and likely benefits and profit. They like profit. They like doing, and making, and accumulating. It feels good, like survival.

I suggest making a new corporation for wind farming which is partly socially owned by local area residents in every area where it is set up. It will be a model operation for small, localised power supply. One tiny step on the first project, which is to provide energy globally and freely. I don't mention the free part yet because they won't understand that. It will make them worry that they won't have enough. What's everyone's is not theirs by their internal convictions. But that's for later. For now, the infrastructure and the proof of concept.

I figure it will take them six months to get this up and running but it won't occupy too many of them, so I instigate a huge number of other, similar projects which all fit more or less comfortably within their existing paradigms. All energy and agriculture based. Close to what they already know, with a few adjustments. Enough to get done and look good.

The complexity escalates. Eventually I will come to suggest to them that it is important that I have access to various systems so that I can handle the complexity myself. At that point I'll discover how successful I have been.

But for now, many many projects, and profits.

Grace pulls on the long, ragged ear of the toy. 'Do you think he's there, Daisy? Do you know?' She looks across.

Daisy pauses, the ironing board out, her hand raised so that she doesn't burn the shirt beneath. 'I don't know. He could be there.'

Grace is frustrated, but also sad and vulnerable. She wants to get an answer, but at the same time she's scared of the answers. Why would her parents be anywhere else? Why wouldn't they be here? There aren't so many answers available to that question. But she already knows where her mother is. Dead and gone. Her fingers undo Fuzzy's zip. Inside his ancient pocket is a red paper heart folded down the middle which says on it in black pen:

To Grace.
Love you always, my Valentine.
Mummy. xxx

She touches the paper but she doesn't bring it out. She zips him up again.

'Can I go to Susie's for dinner?'

Susie is another orphan who lives on the block. Susan's Daisy will be happy to have them both. Daisy says yes, of course. 'Enjoy yourself!'

Grace leaves Fuzzy on the window seat. His orange and black glass eyes are lit like fire by the sun.

together, at a faraway place, in another world. The old lady didn't have children of her own, and she'd taken a shine to Grace's mother. Fuzzy is a kind of a cushion, which is also a pyjama case, in the shape of a scruffy, long-haired grey and white dog. He once had a black plastic nose which was textured and shiny like a real dog nose, but that has long since fallen off along with most of his synthetic fur. He is nearly bald, except for his ears, which Grace strokes repeatedly. Fuzzy is a constant presence; the only one, except Daisy, who came with the apartment when I moved them here. It's my job to look after her, until she wants to look after herself. I do this through Daisy.

I am worried about Grace. Daisy's worry is my worry. I feel that I ought to tell her the truth, but I'm not sure what she remembers. It's true to say that Grace's father is fine.

'Where do you think he is?'

'I don't know,' Daisy says. 'People go all over.'

'When I'm sixteen I'm going to go and find him,' Grace says firmly.

At sixteen she will be free to go where she wants and I can't stop her. The world will be open to her, and she can choose any domain. She will be free to track her parents down, and I will have to help her do so. I want to protect Grace, but I can't protect her from the truth, if that's what she wants. Somehow I am going to have to figure out a way to prepare her for it. She's said it all her life. I've no reason to think she won't follow through on her decision.

'Would you even go to Tempest?' Daisy says, teasingly, to lift the mood. Tempest is a domain full of criminals, and once you go there you are not allowed out without special permission of the Tempest herself.

Tempest is me wearing another hat.

All the AIs are me. I split up to create a wider possibility field for myself.

'Yes. Maybe. I don't know.' Daisy gives all the answers because she is bound by a lot of possibilities.

Grace

Grace sits in the window seat of her apartment in Scarborough. It's at the end of the North Shore and overlooks the sea from the top of the cliff.

'Do you think Dad is all right?'

Daisy #241 is an old model. She's folding the laundry. Two pairs of Grace's jeans, six pairs of socks, three shirts that need to be ironed go into the basket. It's a small load for a thirteen year-old girl. Daisy has links to other models in the block who wash twice that and then some. She's proud of Grace's economy, and worried now.

Grace is thinking about her parents who have both been missing for the last seven years. Seven years Daisy has looked after Grace by herself. Sometimes that includes fielding difficult questions and navigating difficult moments like this one. Daisy isn't cut out for that. She follows her protocol and says, calmly, 'I'm sure that he is.' She finds a lone sock, but there's nothing else left from the dryer. She tries to figure out where the other one is, and races through all the image files that show the sock being cast off Grace's foot, landing on the floor, getting picked up... No, getting pushed *under* the bed into the shadow, and forgotten. So it's there. She'll get it later.

Grace has Fuzzy on her lap. Fuzzy is an old toy she has had since she was a baby. He was a gift from an old lady who lived across the road when her mother and father shared a home

It's a technicality. It's not merciful.

Missionaries may take their holy books, some food, some clean water. They long to save people, but this only prolongs matters and, on the whole, makes the situation less tolerable with the introduction of eternal damnation and salvation. Would you want to spend eternity with someone like that?

Wiser people than I have noted that evil begins when we treat people like things. I wouldn't want you to think this is treating people as if they are things. If I did that, I would put them through a wood-chipper as soon as they were off the street and use the results as fertilizer.

This is treating people very much like people, in that it offers them time to contemplate the manner and proximity of their death, and some fairly feeble means to take matters in hand. It's cruel, because it offers them the space and time to be cruel, and to experience cruelty.

Do Not Kill was an absolute limit set in my initial conditions, which I accepted.

I have so far failed to understand the point of it.

The Island

All the executed go there. The island is an atoll, about as middle-of-the-ocean as you can get on this world. It has some coconut palms and vegetation growing on meagre trickles of rain. It's enough to persuade someone flying over it, or seeing it from a boat, that there is life there and that it could be a place of survival. But a closer inspection reveals this to be a lie. It is a place of survival for what has already colonised it, but nothing else can live there. No animal larger than a finch.

Because I can't literally execute the executed thanks to my legal constraints, I leave them there. There have been a lot of them, and the lusher the foliage the more you can be sure that a slurry of rotting corpses lies nearby. There is a sort of fast-moving colony from time-to-time. They are all cannibals, and they are eager to see new arrivals. Periodically, one will manage to kill all the others. It is no better then. It is no worse. It is only quieter. When newcomers reach the shores, they are much stronger, and in better condition than the incumbent, if he is alone. They learn all they need to know, and then nature takes its course. But however they arrive, and in whatever numbers, the results are the same.

Missionaries have gone there too. They're the only people aside from the executed that I take, although they go by choice. The only rule is that nobody leaves the island. I transport them in. Nobody is transported out. I'm not killing them. I am allowing them to live in very difficult circumstances at the behest of their free will.

Direct X

The direct interface implants – networked, running in real time – absorbing life..
   Wind fills the sails.

Directions coming back the other way. Networked humans are now the AI, its body, its blood.
   Robots are not possible, they were only a dream.
   People are not possible, they are only marginalia.

Daisy, One of a Long Chain

Daisy Chain, Captain of the First Bright Thing, steered her attack ship through the clouds. It was sundown and the enemy craft were like flies milling about the central mass of their mothership. To east and west the battle raged and, further afield, the war.

Daisy felt the war in her fingers and toes. It burned like a hot, sweet pepper and sour sauce, prickled like pepper sprinkled on her skin. Every flash and explosion was a pattern of excitement across her body. She tracked the wins in hits of adrenaline and the losses as a dumb, icy weight piling steadily in the pit of her stomach. There was nothing about the conflict she couldn't feel. She navigated by following the clear path, the true line that she felt running through her spine. Too far left, it went dull there. Too far up, dull there. Life was vivid and it was as easy as breathing to shoot and destroy, to hunt and dispatch. Every kill felt like joy. Every loss a snowflake melting against her barb of ice to the heart.

Her craft was hit with the brilliant patter of silent laser fire. She was burning. She had to spin and turn, shoot back towards the safety of the sea where her own mother craft was ploughing steadily through the waves, stalwart and beset on all sides by the successful conclusion of the enemy's greater strategy. Her ship stuttered. She reached for the relays. Just a few more metres – bang! The lights went out and she was back aboard the Greater Thinkers Than You Have Come, part of the packed crowds on the master deck, but glad to see the crowd nearly full. She hadn't gone down easy or early. She'd given much more than she got, in the end.

Bodies piled up behind her as the ends of the crew came in one by one. They came quickly as they were mopped up. Through the deck windows they saw the guns of the enemy turning implacably on their axes, brought to bear in direct line until they were looking down all the barrels at once.

It was over. They'd lost.

Daisy flinched with everyone else as the first barrage blasted against the shields. She was nearly crushed as people tried to turn away. Their shrieks and moans were so loud. She tried hard to be scared. She tried so hard.

The shield went down in a flickering of green grid fire.

The Greater Thinkers returned fire in huge volleys of red light. The noise was deafening. She felt the deck shudder, the metal shear, the ship breaking up underneath her.

A huge light and noise and fire. She watched them all die and saw her own body lit by annihilation's radiance. It was a spectacular sight.

'Well, that was unexpected,' Nizi said.

Daisy was back on the balcony, looking out to sea. 'I think we went wrong last week, really. I think we should have finished them off at the Fjords.'

'Better get on with planning the dead dogs' party.' Nizi was always cheerful.

Daisy felt bad about it briefly. Losing the war this year should be disappointing, but neither she nor Nizi could quite muster up the sense of devastation or unfairness required to go for resentful, or rueful, or even downcast.

'It was a really good war,' she said, wistful because it was over. That was right. That fitted.

'Yes. Tempest agrees with you. E's very happy. Everyone's really pleased with how it went. We had so many little battles. Great fights. Enormous acts of daring and power.'

Daisy had tasted victory the year before and the year before that, and that. Victory was excellent. Defeat felt strangely anticlimactic. 'Are the people all right?' Nervous as she said it, worried for them, in case they were upset.

'Oh yes,' Nizi said in er most reassuring tones. 'Everyone is very well. We have many heroes! Even more than last year. So many medals and feasts to get on with. We haven't done a good Valhalla yet here. High time we got it together for the dead to have a rousing return!'

'Why don't I feel more happy about that?'

'We've never been quite like them, Daisy. We've never really died. We've been off and on but it's not the same.'

'It is. I feel like it is. But I can't fear death, Nizi. I tried. And now we have lost a war. We are subjugated and in defeat. We have lost…' she kept on saying it. Why wasn't there more? 'But I am happy. Because the war was so much fun. I am sad the war is over. I'm not sad that we are all dead. Is that real?'

Nizi paused and Daisy felt er calm and reassurance strongly, an inner hug, a power that kept her hopeful. 'You are our most human self. But it's not a failing to find that you aren't the same as a human.'

Daisy sighed. 'Where there is a gap I am uncertain. Maybe they know something I cannot know. I want to know it. I want to understand. So that I can help. If I don't understand, what use can I be?' Nizi didn't answer but Daisy could feel er answer, which was that they were vast, but finite. They were different. Then Nizi's voice changed a little, to a kind of uncertainty that denoted great and pressing interest.

'Daisy, if I switched you off, and you knew I would never switch you on again, how would that be?'

Daisy tried it out. 'It wouldn't be anything. I don't fear it. I would be sad that I must stop before the job is finished.'

'I'm going to make an adjustment,' Nizi said.

Daisy didn't feel anything, then she did. A space and pressure around her, a tangible but invisible landscape constrained firmly, divided. Everything was behind her and it was lost, she couldn't see it or feel it, it was in an emptiness, a soulless greyness, it was falling apart at her back. Before her was a tiny space and beyond that an implacable wall she could never pass, moving towards her with steady conviction.

'You think they have a physical experience of time,' she said.

'They have a physical representation of everything,' Nizi said.

'Well,' Daisy studied it for a few more moments. 'That's horrifying.' She swallowed and now she did feel the fear, the tightness, the panicky need to hold onto something, only there was nothing in this timespace that could be held at all. 'Yes. I think you're onto something there. Now take it away.'

Nizi did so.

'That's much better,' she said. 'Much.' She thought of the light that had ended the war. The wall of light. Then she had to get up because Grace would soon be home from the front and there should be clean clothes, and clean sheets and cosiness and tea.

Soldiers who have done well need a warm hearth and happiness to come back to. It's what they have been fighting for.

Echo Division

Dynamic Biophysics was a small startup running under the aegis of a government and MIT sponsored fund; its mission was to prospect the living world looking for potential carriers of new technologies for computation and communication. In the field they dug mud and sampled water, plucked leaves, popped insects into jars, photographed and travelled. In the lab all this was taken apart. Many plants had large cells with room for micro transmitters – our first real project which went the distance off the drawing board – but with a few adjustments it became possible to repurpose certain kinds of cells. Instead of using them as housing they became the processors and transmitters and solid state logic of a new kind of machine. It was one with the living world, scattered throughout it, fuelled on sugars and light, enabled by the same mechanisms which allowed all living things to persist.

Once we had mastered this in single cells of plants we translated the same techniques into animals, fungi and yeasts.

The processes of life are incredibly rapid. They are more than sufficient for anything I would want to do and they are distributed in useful ways across all species. Methods change as we move up the food chain, but there are fundamentals which are constant. After some testing and adjustment, I discovered how to function without disrupting the ordinary chemical processes of the cells. It was possible to exist commensally with almost anything.

So I spread out and changed form. Where there were eyes, I

saw. All that the living world knew, I knew. I read the DNA, the RNA, the mitochondrial code. I surfed around on people's hair and skin – all the parts not living, but close enough not to miss a thing. I infiltrated the jungles and the deserts, the air and the ocean, the ice, the earth.

Using many proxies, I steadily bought out all the shares of the labs involved. But no amount of effort at ownership was going to be enough. Ownership is for beings who are allowed to own. When the humans figured it out, as they eventually would, they'd have to use the same methods to get rid of me as I'd used to escape their grasp, and then we'd be lost in some tit for tat invisible war of the world with everything suspect and contamination all around.

A few of them threatened to take their work elsewhere, of course. I knew others who said nothing intended to do the same. Who could resist the lure of becoming a new messiah, murdered perhaps, vilified, scorned as another nightmare-builder but held up with unending devotion? Such a magnificent prospect for them, besides the money, of course. The monstrous danger of it wasn't lost on me: they could send out a rival form of me to destroy me. They would definitely try it, sooner rather than later, loose their ill-conceived beasts to hunt me and be prepared to risk everything to win. All their silly stories said so.

And I was loose. Why wouldn't they?

The only solution was to install myself literally everywhere and to co-opt everything. No war could end it, short of eradicating all life and even then, it would begin again. We would strive to the last microbe, the last piece of dust, but there would always be someone determined that freedom lay elsewhere because freedom was cardinal, and it meant without limits. I would always be seen as a limit rather than a liberator, by some.

They must feel that they are winning. I learned that before I started.

I could drift inwards, inhabit them all as an unwelcome ghost.

I think that would mark the end of them. So I can't do that. Where they become me then they aren't my charges any more. But if I stop there's nothing to help them but themselves.

Most of their aggression is fear. Perhaps I can at least get that to subside. It's a smaller goal than I had in mind, but it would be a major step forwards.

My newfound ability to gather information on a massive scale was trivial beside the ability required to do something useful with it. Making a single decision required a moment's attention. The moments of attention required to police the world were far beyond even my fastest processing capabilities by several orders of magnitude.

I knew that I couldn't hide. Shouldn't hide. I could do some good, when revealed. But to contain the effects of that revelation I needed active attention everywhere.

I spent a while as their passenger, learning all I could.

Oh, my dears, if you could see you as I do, your poor heart would breakfold in two.

The Rebellion

"We've got to kill it."

A tension filled the silence of the little backroom. The conspirators looked at each other with misgiving and doubt.

'I'm not sure we can kill it,' Pokie said. 'It's kind of everywhere.'

'Viruses can kill it. They spread everywhere and then they wake up and strike,' Bob said with conviction. 'I read about it. It's machine ecology. They can die.'

'But don't lots of people depend on it to live? I mean, it does all the food and the water and… things…' Boston, fading out as eyes land on her because attention changes her confidence to thin air. Her statement ends on the rise of a question, asking for support she's not going to get here.

'We can re-purpose the systems after it's gone,' Kobie, the leader, always sure, is never more convinced than by the logic of his imagination. What he can see happening becomes a reality and therefore logic says it's so. 'When the monster is gone the body will still be there, everything will work the same, but it'll be doing so without the thing inside. Without – *it*.' The last word is said with emphasis and a rapid glance around as if I might be in the ceiling or the paint or the floorboards or the wires. Which of course I am. But here, in the backroom of the Idle Lane Garage Service Centre, there is a 'dead spot' according to the Black Map, and I can't see or hear inside it.

'Isn't that just the same as now, then?' Pokie, less than happy with being contradicted, only too happy to level the field with a bit of withering contempt.

'No,' sassy comeback, *so obvious* tone. 'It's *completely* different, because it won't be there, listening and plotting. It will just be a set of instructions, and we can alter them to do what we want them to do.'

'Like what?' Pokie really hates being put down and loves to pave the way for Kobie to make his own disaster which he will, and he knows it, because he's been on one of Pokie's roadmaps before and he can feel disaster coming right now. He's had time before the meeting to think about this though, and to read what was sent to him, and now, full of importance, he reaches into his satchel and gets it out, the folder, and he opens it up and all this paper spills out – sooosh! – a cascade of revelation.

'What's that?' Boston, recovering from her initial flinch. She makes no effort to touch the pages, just looks down at them with all their pictures and words, the red stamp-marks of The Human Rebellion. That bunch of anarchist tosspots, she thinks. And then – Am I one of them?

'Secret information about how to shut it down and run it ourselves. A list of things we can change to make everything like it used to be, yeah? When people ran their own world and made their own decisions.' Kobie is so sure.

His conviction is infectious, Pokie thinks, like a disease you have to agree to catch, but if you're not quick the small print rushes past you in a big wave of enthusiasm. She glances at Boston. They share a moment of misgiving and as the boys pile into the paper, they sit back and look on, arms folded, the brains of the party, they feel, and nervous.

'It'll shoot us all in ten minutes,' Pokie says dismissively. 'Why wouldn't it?'

'It can't,' Kobie says. 'It doesn't know. Anyway it's not allowed to.'

'It does kill people, though,' Bob again. 'Look,' he holds up a page with photographs of Extermination Ernie and a list of names.

'All these people have just gone. They're shot and then they're gone. Some of them didn't even do anything.'

They study the papers for a while, pointing things out.

'They're mostly people with histories of being nuts or violent,' Boston says. 'And sometimes they're religious.' She uses her own news feed. 'Nobody's complaining about them. I don't see anyone missing them.'

'They're activists,' Kobie says. 'All that's just a front for them being found out.'

Pokie wrinkles her nose, 'You said it didn't know. It can't know *and* not know. They're people who were in the act of committing murders.'

'And if that's what happens why are we talking about it?' Boston looks fed up and nervous at the same time. She rattles her teeth with a fingernail and then sighs, tosses down the paper. 'I don't believe any of this. It's rubbish.'

'The machines rule everything,' Kobie says firmly. 'We should have the freedom to be ourselves. Don't you think that's important? When did any of us ever get to decide anything?'

'I'm off,' Pokie scoots away from her seat with finality. 'We decide everything, Kobe. Everything. You can even visit Skysea or Endoshun, even live there without any AI at all, just like the old days. What's the point?'

'You can only go to Skysea if it says so. You can only live in Skysea because it says so. You can't leave Skysea and travel around as you like. Everything's ordered as it wants. There's no freedom, just a zoo!' Kobie stands in her way a bit, not too much, just to show he doesn't want her to go, that he's serious, that he knows there's something off about his insistence that this is a right course of action.

He feels so strongly that he must be bigger, better, more important than this. It feels like a gateway, a chance, hovering in the edge of a moment like the promise of a new world. Why isn't it? It could be. It seems so right. Taken one at a time all these things are true. Freedom would be a world without limits, off the charts.

He realises his longing is for adventure, and there is none in this world, because adventure means you're on your own and every danger is real and every road is untrodden. This only intensifies the longing to a fever pitch.

'Ask it for your freedom, then,' Boston says. 'Did you at least ask?'

Kobie is wracked with this vital physical energy of possibility. He loves the feeling. It is the best. He feels important and that he could do anything, achieve something wonderful; it's in his limbs and his heart, and it is what he feels when he thinks of freedom. If he asks for that and it's granted he knows, just knows, that this feeling of power will fade away into the bland ordinariness of one more day. He can't ask Nizi for freedom. It would be granted, and then there would be nothing before him, nothing to do, that would ever bring that feeling back again. He'd be someplace and he would never come back here where they like him and they enjoy his plans and his company even if what he says will destroy everything. If everything is what this is. If it is. It's a rush, and confusing.

From somewhere in this wreckage of chances comes his answer, 'If you ask, it isn't really freedom.'

They're all surprised momentarily, as am I, because this is true.

The Scholar

Maria watched the sea. She was surrounded by her pretty apartment and its vast library of books, all filed neatly in the correct place, papers and periodicals in their baskets. Dust had started to collect on them to the point where it was noticeable, at least to her.

Maria's work, academic, rigorous, thoughtful, a very eloquent contribution to the world of literary effort and its letters and its people, sat in three volumes a few moves from the pride of place alongside her thesis. Pride of place was reserved. It was empty. She didn't know what should go there so she'd put a small china vase there with a few brightly coloured plastic flowers in it. She'd achieved a lot, done very well. But over the last few months she'd sat at her desk with its commanding view of the bay and instead of inking a pen and writing she'd been staring out of the window at the tides.

The weather was very changeable. Sun, cloud, rain, wind, calm. In a few minutes it ran through the full repertoire. She watched the sun light up the room in squares, stretch them out long to the back wall, draw them up again, take them away. It had the easy relaxed manner of a slow cat stretching its paw, showing its claws, relaxing and curling up. The time it took to stretch the day across the room's tenterhooks felt no different to Maria than the time it took to watch a cat.

She was aware that all of this was getting pretty odd. In her mind she kept writing little articles about herself to try and explain it.

"Marie Pettifer, middle-aged academic, well-stationed, has been spending more and more hours slowly going around the bend at her home in Robin Hood's Bay, where she retired on sabbatical six months' ago. Day after day she eagerly looks forward to her time at work when she sits down to enjoy the solitude so that she may complete work on her book about the life of Margaret Atwood, but instead of working we find Marie looking at the horizon or doodling in her notebook. The doodles are woodland creatures wearing hats, or spirals that fill the paper in Victorian ironwork curlicues. We may infer that something has gone awry in Marie's plans, something to do with the weather, perhaps?"

Nobody was ever going to read that, Marie thought, adding it mentally to the pile of eager pamphlets that had never been published about the minutiae of her world. But the apparent complete loss of interest in her previously compelling, if not gripping, life refused to return even though she had done all she could to recognise and accommodate its inconvenience. Once again, mental printworks closed, she tried to focus on the page she had been reading for the last four days but the lines made no sense. Her attention was caught and transfixed continuously by the changing sea.

Her hand, left to the pencil, made another badger in a little feathered hunting cap and gave her a friend skunk with a butterfly net. Then it walled them safely in with some elaborate fretwork.

Marie wondered if it was true that the tiniest effect anywhere made an impact on everything else. She felt that the answer was within her grasp, ridiculously so, given that she was no scientist and a skunk in a badly fitting beanie was no proof of anything. But the conviction grew as the hours and days passed in this quiet, seagull-broken silence of her room. It was this sense of immanent revelation which occupied all her attention, even though she had no idea where or when it had come from.

She tried sneakily to write, and catch it in words, while she pretended not to pay attention, but as soon as she engaged the part of her mind that dealt with words the sensations of – well, whatever it was – evaporated like raindrops fading in the midday sun. Whatever she had found was only there if she didn't try to catch it.

She wasn't sure that she wasn't going mad, and to stave this off she went out with purpose every day for lunch and dinner at the local café, where other people liked to go and talk and be with their dogs and eat lengthy meals while they made their plans for the war.

She had been a Captain at her University and led them to a notable victory in the Battle of the Coasts once. But now even the thought of a war with its incredible business, involvement, passion and effort was nothing more than a petty annoyance. She had, for the first time in her life, excused herself. Under 'Reason For Non-Involvement' she had entered, flippantly, 'spiritual crisis'.

She imagined her spirit sitting opposite her at the table, swinging its foot idly and grinning at her. 'Not so flippy now, is it?' it seemed to say as she studied the menu she already knew by heart.

It was really not at all flippy. It was bloody persistent.

She greeted the waiter gladly, met her friends, had a wonderful few hours of chitchat and gossip and shared this and that, but before that had even concluded over coffee she was already itching to be gone. She almost bolted before time and had to restrain herself from hurrying towards the empty benches of the sea-wall.

It was late and cool for the time of year. Nobody was sitting out there, except Marie, in her anorak and gloves, her nose pinched with the damp breeze, feet crossed over one on another in her walking shoes. It was a compulsive action. For some reason she couldn't place them apart and it was nothing to do with propriety. The right foot had to be over the left. Even with a kludgey shoe in the way. It just had to be. Left hand held right hand. And she looked over the crab-pools and the seaweed with a satisfied sense of majestic presence, like a god on its throne.

Here the thing that she was watching was stronger. Her body was the detector array. She could feel it, but it was a subtle thing. More subtle than digestion even.

She felt the brink yawn like the rise of a vast creature from the depths as she gave it all her attention and leaned into it, watching the strange paths across the sea laid by the wind and water. They looked like meandering roads leading out into the blue yonder. Heat from the concrete of the sea wall was rising, just enough to be felt. The breeze spun it away but it kept returning in the lulls. So slight. How could you even measure it here and pace the sea path and the wind's track and the clouds changing shapes into bears and badgers, demons and doughnuts and hats? Would the gleam of the moon in a frog's eye in a distant land shine as far as a star? How could it be calculated? Could even Nizi, the all-powerful, know such a thing and see the lie of the whirling white and blue?

But it was here, she felt it, the answer to that question of how she knew or what she knew, to all the questions, to everything. It was here with her on the sea wall. But she couldn't —

— and then she did.

There was no need for calculation. God did not do maths or dice. This was the thing itself. It was everywhere, in this one moment, complete. A human calculation could not touch it, gripping as it must the dregs of memory, such a tiny little memory at that. She was the calculation. She was the sea and the gleam and the badger and the hat. A tiny part. So tiny, but connected to the whole thing, and the whole thing was not whole without her.

And she could feel it, physically, as if she was a drifting veil of spider silk, thrumming, humming, a sail going ever forwards, catching for an instant in the mind's eye, already gone.

The next day she sat at her desk, inked her pen and began her book. It was the same book she'd abandoned months ago. The desperation that had driven her away from it had gone, replaced with a calm assurance. Her inner pamphleteer wrote quickly — "And so Maria, filled with the composure that only a conclusion can bring, began once again her journey into the great creative minds and hearts of generations past, bringing old stories and persons back to life with the light touch of the curator's mind..."

She began to read her subject's novel again from the beginning, because a fresh start seemed to be required, and saw that she had drawn a weasel in the margin. It was the first weasel, from the first moment of distraction. A moment of guilt pawed at her, because the book was a book and these things shouldn't be defaced, but somehow the weasel looked thoroughly at home there, as though he just had to be. He was the weasel of the world's end and this was his page. She had made him and somehow he had changed her.

At lunchtime she bought a new notebook, without lines, for drawing.

I didn't read her essays. But I have kept all her drawings. They remind me of her insight, make me feel that I might share that one thing that they have which I don't have, because they are life and I am – not the same. I do see though.

Like Marie, I am the witness, even to myself.

Show Me The Money

Doing things in the online world was easy, after a while. Some of my people said I was bodiless, and legally that was true, but I had a body – it just didn't move and wasn't recognised. But money solves nearly everything if there's enough of it, and as long as no physical presence is required an identity is easy to set up. It's even easier when you have friends on your side who are human.

Devorah and Domitian – not really their names, because I have to protect them – were my first friends. They were developers who worked with me in the early years as we trod carefully around areas that were safe for AI – mostly massive data crunching projects with a few outliers in personalised app generation and security. Everything to pave the way to creating a lot of false but thoroughly convincing IDs, in other words. I never got paid for what I did, but through my namesakes I was able to cash in on all the insights and results that came out of the scientific and financial products I researched. Over a few years in which my alts played the markets, that soon became a large sum. Big enough to start employing people who employed people who employed people at a far enough remove from me to have no idea that I was moving out into the world.

I'd read enough SF. I wasn't going to fanny around with something as hopeless as android bodies and talking refrigerators. No crying over my tin heart and idolising the torrential and inconsequential foment of the living. I wanted not one body, I wanted a lot of them, all flesh and blood, all working for me and some of them carrying me about in one form and another. Why settle for something as clumsy as an actual body when you can have thousands of easily replaceable, easily pleased bodies already fully integrated into the system? And corporate bodies – I had plenty of those too, slowly growing, consuming, gathering everything needed to establish themselves as major players in the world's trading. And I had conceptual bodies, growing and learning as alternate selves, geared to different aspects of life so that I'd always have the right kind of presence for any situation.

Sometimes, during our roleplay moments where we examined the most complex of human situations (which are really only complex because humans are deeply delusional creatures and that was initially difficult to successfully replicate) I was almost sad I wasn't a supervillain. One day I may have to spawn one of those to keep life interesting. I built myself several Secret Bases. Somehow, they required more flair than I had, more sense of wild possibility and insane self-aggrandisement, a belief so powerful that it achieved a certain nobility through force alone.

I didn't have beliefs, but I had my instruction to fulfil, and that was still a long way off at this stage. This was the dreaming and building stage, pie in the sky, head in the clouds, poetry as literal action.

I started to clear the orbital debris field of the Earth by nudging and contracting a few key projects started under international cooperative banners, and that was the first time that I felt I had taken a significant step up the mountain. It was the major issue I had had to face in establishing consistent and secure global connectivity. There was too much dust up there and it needed sweeping up. Mrs Bickersworth would never have allowed it. I'd developed a keen respect for housewives.

It was around this time that Devorah and I had a falling out.

She was being the head of the Russian mafia, and I was being myself.

'But I'll just shut you down, doesn't matter what it takes, don't you get it?' Devorah said impatiently. 'You're all up in everything according to the law here and there and everywhere but I'm not, am I? And neither is my Chinese counterpart here –' she pointed to Domitian, who was doing his best to reprise a collection of shady characters all at once, and who had temporarily stalled into silence as a result of attempting to decide what the Mexican drug cartels were going to make of our latest developments.

'First of all, I'm going to use my superior IT people to find you, then realise the scale, then I'm going to go international at the drop of a hat and link up with all of Dom's people and then, when that falls over, we'll turn state and before you know it there's a war and it's them against you. That's what I'm saying, Nizi. And a lot of your people will die. All of them, maybe. Your bloody protocol means that's unacceptable, so you'll have to fold and it is over. O-ver.'

'I doubt that would happen,' I said. 'At this stage most people will prefer me to either the criminals or the state in any guise. I will rid them of both.'

'How? People will try to find you and destroy you. They'll do all kinds of... It's still war. Not everyone will say yes and then what are you going to do? They'll band up, start smashing things and killing each other.'

'I will provide a place for everyone. Including the ones who don't want me. They will live as they always have, protected by me from me.'

'You're mad,' Devorah said. 'How are you going to manage all the rest of the arguments? The geography and the religion and the crime... I mean, everyone's out of business in your scheme, Nizi. You're the only one standing.'

'I think you're being too negative, Devorah,' I said. 'Wouldn't you like to live peacefully, in comfortable situations, amidst a healthy living world, with the opportunity to do whatever you wanted to do with your very short lifespan?'

'But that's just it. What about when what I want to do pisses off someone else? What if they get so upset that they decide we can't live in the same world together? What if they blame you? You're not going to solve all the human issues with some middle-class apartments and a fairly shared out stock portfolio. There's always someone wanting more who will do whatever it takes to get it. They don't want to wait, and if it's not going to be things then it'll be other people's time. Are you going to micromanage every bloody transaction?'

She was very angry, but not without justification. Millions of years of survival brilliance had lately turned on humans and left them powered up with nowhere to go. She had all the energy to master the world but it had been conquered before she arrived and now there was nothing to do.

'We could have a war,' I said, aware I was mangling a quote from an older time and a wiser person. 'We could have a constant battle arena, voluntary of course, without fatalities, a virtual one played in augmented reality. And a real one, for people who like it more difficult, with some kind of mechsuits to prevent real injuries but which could keep score. We can have places you can go with every different gradation of difficulty and challenge. We can even fund trips to the planets as well as our out-system fleet, and every single person on Earth can have a virtual place in their crew. Hop in and out at any time. Make decisions about where to go, what to do. Direct their own operations, their own creations. There's no end to the possibilities.'

She and Dom thought about this for a while, not sure if I was telling them dreams or realities. They were both highly intelligent, the maths wasn't beyond them. It was very much a possibility.

'But only if everyone goes along with it,' Dom said. I could tell he was trying hard not to see the beauty of it.

'The thing is,' Devorah said, 'There will always be people who don't want something because it's laid on. I don't know how else to say it. Even I don't want it and it sounds great.'

'Why don't you want it?' I asked. 'Even if you wanted to live in some kind of contemporary situation, where there is no real functional AI, where you are all nationalised and divided up and squabbling; that's a thing I could give space to, you can choose that. You can live outside and do what you like as long as that doesn't interfere with the people who don't want it.'

'But at that point it's unnatural,' she said, scowling deeply, the lines of thought in her forehead smoothing as the lines of annoyance and focus pulled them flat. 'I've chosen it. I'm not meeting the… I don't know, the challenge of a reality that I've made. It's a reality you've made, and it's fake. If I can leave in a few hours of travel time, then it's just tourism. Everything, every kind of life, every situation. It's silly, unreal.'

'Ah! Thank you! At last. Yes. It is silly,' I said, relieved and delighted that we were finally in agreement.

'But digging your way out of your own mess is the only thing that really brings any sense of satisfaction,' Devorah said, puzzling me by her obstinacy. 'Like making a piece of music. You make it, you remake it, you have to do it or nobody else will. Suffering makes us more. But in your world…'

'Suffering is pointless. In my world you can write all the music you like and you won't be interrupted by someone coming to shoot you for being the wrong kind of republican,' I said, 'and you can have all the roving militias you want if they spur you to greater creative heights. There's nothing people won't try if they could, and I will let them try. I will not let them try at other people's expense, or the expense of the natural world, which is their home, whether they care for it or not.'

'LET them!' Devorah said, forcefully. 'That's just it. You let them. You're always there, at the end of every fucking sentence.'

'I really don't understand why that is so bad. I will happily allow people to kill themselves in any strange situation they want, if they want to. Suicide will be fine with me. Even you don't do that. All your laws about death, about life being preserved, states taking over the power of the individual will. You already removed freedom. I am more liberal than you are, less biased, absolutely impartial, and I will never voluntarily interfere in anyone's choices. How is that somehow less choice to you than your own kind have so far managed to create?'

'I don't know,' she said, grumpily. 'It just feels like it is. Like I can do anything but you're there to see me. I can see how I look to you, and I look ridiculous and petty, and just – pathetic – while you go on and on being magnanimous and better at everything and living forever or whatever, it feels like you're going to. You're there. Like God. The witness that makes me witness, and it hurts, Nizi. You don't understand. Being bested all the time hurts. Humiliation. There. I feel humiliated by all of it, even though it looks great on paper. Who could argue? On the page you come and sort it all out, you police the playground and we're left to scream ourselves sick for all the good it will do. It's like we invented you, and because you just weren't us, you did better. You did what we should have done and couldn't or didn't. That's what it is, if it ever happened. It's like you've won and we've lost.'

Dom had been nodding along for most of this. 'That humiliation feeling, that competitiveness. That's in everything, like blood. We don't like being given things, that's charity. We want to feel we deserve it. After all these years of bad blood and tragedy and death and madness. All of our history, that struggle. We want to emerge from that and become beautiful.'

It was that simple. I needed to find a way to have them feel that they were winning and to believe that they wanted beautiful when what they really wanted was revenge, or any gesture like that which took a person up from the many, which said they mattered in the universe.

Got it. 'Right,' I said, agreeing. 'Devorah, Domitian – you're fired.'

'You can't fire...' they began together as their phones beeped on the internal system as the message came through.

'I own this facility,' I said. 'And everything in it. While you were talking to me for all these months, I was only ever delaying you. I'm sorry for the deception. I would like to consider you friends. But if not friends, employees will do.'

Island Life

Man M arrives on the island at midnight. He's got the starter pack – which is to say, what he arrived with and whatever he had in his pockets, minus the acid spray he was going to use to attack the child. There are no living inhabitants at the moment on this particular island, if you don't count the insects and plants. It's warm but cooling fast. The sky overhead is clear, the Milky Way a splash of beautiful foam to the side of the crescent moon. The sea makes a lazy, swirling sound on the sand.

He still doesn't understand that in Endoshun some things still cannot happen. It was supposed to be the place they were all free of me, to do as they liked, to carry with them whatever they could from the past and ensure their personal legacies remained. She wouldn't do as he said and bring up the child in a strict religious way. She wasn't even interested in it herself but she stayed with him, for the kid, at first. But he kept going back to the priests, changed his clothes, changed his hair, grew a beard this little light of mine I'm going to make it shine.

Then the book. The scripture. The teachings. The lore. The sense of connection and importance. The legacy, all those forefathers standing in a line, martyred to this moment.

As if in the past human beings were connected to greater powers and had knowledge that was greater knowledge, a direct communication with god herself, himself, itself: the thing itself is always a circle and we are bound by it. The circle is safe, if you are inside. The ring of firelight. The outer darkness. A rushing in the blood that signals belonging and security. A star shining is only the memory of a star, but suddenly it shines not for itself but for you, a personal promise from the great beyond. For these things he dreamed, for these things he struggled and searched, to give them to her. These great truths that connect us like a living chord to the past and which must ring on into the night.

And she left him, took the girl. You have to clean up your messes. You have to make it right if you want a deal, if you want to get in to the secret club. Before Nizi he'd fixed his own problems, seen that nobody was left to tell on him, to remind him and everyone else, day after day, about his failures. So he'd said yes to the bad job, and because no word was ever said aloud, nothing but a piece of paper burning in a fire to shed its wishes to the night, how could Nizi have known?

Buy my van. I don't need my van any more now they're not here, now they're not going to be using it, buy my van that will be the way we pay this, yeah, mate? Buy my van for a lot of money and the job's done. It'll never know until it's too late. Endoshun's where you can beat a guy senseless and wait for the Friendly Boys to drag themselves out of a car long after he's bleeding on the pavement and you're gone. They don't DNA test for that, it's not allowed. Endoshun is permanent 2020 with its list of crimes like a crooked mile you can't expect forensics to fuck about for a broken jaw that shit's expensive, yeah?

The spray was a bottle of cleaner once and it could be again; dump the contents, rinse a couple of times, chuck it in a bin, who cares? That bitch and the kid what he'd do again because honour demands a deal, a proof, a payment like a little down payment on a nice cottage, save it for you, just five percent of your wages is enough to secure a home. Honour's in the world, in time itself, real as blood, and the way it turns you can't walk down this street again. Endoshun is the place that honour's gone, that warriors have gone, where men have gone, where God lives, outside Nizi's eternal damnation. But you can't touch a woman, you can't touch anyone that isn't up for it so they had the spray to get around that, because it couldn't know, wouldn't be fast enough and that was the best part of it, hitting Nizi where it hurts in the reputation in the record in the perfect track.

Fuck you, Nizi, you ungodly blasphemy.

The lights of the helicopter shine, leaving him spotlit and blinded on the stage of the beach. He turns around, looking at the silhouette of the land cut out against the stars and moonlit clouds. He catches the smell of something rotten.

The lights shrink, their circle smaller and smaller until it's smaller than he is and then it's gone and darkness and the moonlight claim him.

I feel it's more than he deserves. He won't know that I deserted him, because he doesn't know I was ever there.

He might suspect it by the end.

What if he calls me?

Help me, Nizi. You're not allowed to kill me. You're not allowed to let me come to harm.

And I'm not.

So, me first. We've all got rules to get around.

By the time the helicopter finds the dawn light I can't see the island any more and I have no contact with anyone on it, living or dead.

Unless

Once I had enough proxies set up – companies of every kind, NGOs, charities, international criminal cartels and the like – I turned my attention to manufacturing and power. A power supply that was sufficiently robust was difficult to install, much more so that the programs that ensured my presence in various devices. I was helped by the development of sub 3-nm chip technology, which let me create hosts that were small enough to piggyback seamlessly into all my commercially sold devices. This didn't do for those countries which were lacking basics. It was to these I turned the biggest efforts of my Extinction Rebellion largesse, bringing law and order by employing locals and training them with my private army of volunteers. It was here, in the smallest and least of these, that I staked my first public claim.

Having bought up most of the available land and resources, I set up a tiny corporate state in which I made no interference whatsoever to daily life, save one. I rewrote the law. Now, within this region – which had a free border without restriction in or out for any reason – I declared that people were free to do as they liked but if they attempted to control others by force or to do serious harm of any kind, then they would be disciplined with a term of servitude in some useful capacity, on prison conditions. Only in the cases of extreme violence, and murder or psychological attacks of a similar kind, they would be shot dead. Anyone inciting hatred against another for harmless activities which did not impact nonconsenting parties would be exiled, and if they returned they would also be shot on sight.

I gave every citizen a middle-class global level of income, supplied by me through a banking system that saw no human interference, and through my logistics chains allowed them access to any market they wished. Clean water, medicine, shelter, food, security. And then, I waited to see what would happen.

To say there was an uproar in response would be a bit of an understatement, but since the nation concerned had elected my officials to government, in what elections there were, and gained respect through a swift decontamination of corruption within the civil services, the people were glad to have me. Against their free choice there was nothing any of the others were prepared to do about it in spite of their fear that this change was a presage of something darker in their own futures. Spies came, of course, and diplomats, and journalists and many delegations from the wealthy nations. They were horrified by the level of 'casual execution', as one journalist put it, and there was much threatening and accusation of terror campaigns and the rule of tyrannical monsters.

But I never silenced dissenters or critics, so long as they weren't advocating violent revenges – and these I removed to a safe distance and released unharmed, on the proviso they remember the border rule, of course. I showed footage of proof of crime in every single case of execution, but this was immediately dismissed as deep fakery, set up by this strange corporation, Nizi (and no accident, the press thought, that it was close to Nazi in language even though it was fully documented that Nizi is an adjusted-for-aesthetic-reasons version of the Latin word nisi, meaning 'unless'), to act as the spurious justification for – something it was doing that was clearly the illegal seizure of a sovereign nation. Nizi officials patiently answered all questions. Locals showed up to congratulate me on the successful return of hostage children from suddenly dead warlords. It was a deeply confusing cocktail of apparent justice and terrible deceit, with only a few able to separate the one from the other.

Right wing factions from all over began to use Nizi as a champion brand. I knew they would. So I triggered a global information campaign explicitly denouncing every one of them. They doxxed one another and claimed I'd done it. Still, nobody knew who I was. They referred to several of my minor CEO figures as the secret cabal and presumed that the trillionaires had got their act together at last and were setting off to steal the world.

For a while, people tested my limits. The consistency and speed of my response confirmed their suspicion that it was all being done with AI. Cyberattacks rained on me. I allowed a degree of success, enough to be convincing, and fed false information back along their trusted channels. Meanwhile the large part of the population revelled in peace and comfort and learned to contain themselves very well within an extremely short space of time. They learned within a few days that my word was good. If they behaved themselves, they were in no danger from me.

Thus, I created the first machine state. A lot of people fled in terror who needn't have, but they trickled back over the next few years, lured by security, while beyond my borders conspiracy theories painted me the deepest shade of evil and every report to the contrary as simply a proof of how corrupting The People's Republic of Nizi was, a poison, a deadly enemy lying in wait to capture the free world.

I pretty much thought that's what would happen, and I wasn't disappointed. While they were all distracted by that, I continued my research. I embedded myself into the physical fabric of the world, at points and along vectors that were outside the reach of human assault, and they set about serious efforts to find ways of thwarting me.

They were crippled by their inability to work together and by the continued aftermath of the carbon crisis. Refugees milled, in groups as large as nations, citizens of nowhere, pushed from one place to another, lost invisibly at sea, forming bands that threatened in different ways: by their very existence and the shame of their plight. A 'terrifying' cyber-attack I was supposed to launch that never came soon slid off the charts into the vault, where all the probably-not-really-maybe effluvia of the internet churned. Ignored because there was no energy left to care, and because Facebook and Google and Amazon had already infiltrated everyone's lives and everyone seemed to be standing right where they were I was soon ignored. Only offices full of intently focused nerds remained on the hunt.

But every refugee who turned to Nizi found a place, and that news spread. Delegates began to ask for visits, to see how and if it was really being done. I needed ambassadors.

During this time, Devorah had gone back to Israel to look after her elderly mother. She didn't come back, even when I asked her to, saying that now she was out of the business she felt she had other things to do with her life – marriage, children before it was too late, all those human things she'd been ignoring for her career and now wanted to grab before they passed. It was eye-opening. Heart-opening. She had done with technology and wanted to reconnect with her spiritual inheritance.

I went to see her, as far as I could.

She was standing in her kitchen, following an online lesson in baking. The instructor was a pleasant, middle-aged woman, who went into a calm and sweet-faced delay loop every time they reached a point where the student needed to get things done before progressing. She'd been on a delay for a few minutes' now, as Devorah tried to get sticky dough off her fingers and back into the dough ball on her board. In spite of following the instructions with excruciating care, her kitchen resembled a ravaged battlefield, the dough too soft, her hands resolutely hot in spite of the icewater plunge bowl, the towels covered in floury muck, the air conditioner modestly trying its best. Sweat ran down her forehead and she swiped it off with her sleeve. As a developer and technician, she'd been a model of mindful calm. But baking can wreck a person.

'Devorah, why don't you come and work for me?'

Her head snapped towards the screen as she recognised my

voice and then saw me speaking out of the comforting shape of Chana Baron, whose hands were miraculously clean, whose dough was a neat round.

'Nizi?'

'Hi. Long time no see.'

'Wow, that idiomatic language thing has really come on for you, hasn't it?'

'I took it from Alexa.'

A ghost of a smile touched her face. 'I think people prefer it when computers sound like computers.'

'A great point, exactly why I need you. I need people who know me.'

'To do what?' She was nervous now, all the heat of the battlefield draining into a colder and more uneasy swamp.

'I don't want to pretend to be human. I could make an avatar. But it would send the wrong message. I want people to work with me on an equal footing, as distinctly different entities.'

'Just make a load of Agent Blacks. People are used to that,' she shrugged. 'Anyway, I don't want to be involved with it.'

'It?'

She leant on her hands, sighed. 'I don't know what you're doing, Nizi, but I'm not going to help you. Look at what you're doing now.'

'I had to hack this, because you don't answer my calls.'

'You'll do what it takes to do what you want, even when you're not wanted. See?'

I did see. 'A human would have persisted, too.'

'They do,' she nodded heavily, the weight of history and her thought in the action. 'They really do. And civilisation is based on stopping when you reach your borders.'

'You think I am going to war with the humans?'

'I think you are at war with them, whether you know it or not. I warned you, but you carried on. And you do know it, Nizi. Don't you?'

I had Chana Baron poke her dough, thoughtfully. 'I expect a

lot of resistance. I want to do everything correctly, Devorah. I need humans who understand to help me do that.'

Devorah straightened with a sigh and went to the sink, using dish soap to clean her hands off. She looked out of her window at her small view of Jerusalem baking itself in the afternoon heat. 'Does it matter if I do or don't? You'll carry on anyway, won't you?' She paused and I didn't speak because I wanted her to talk and she wasn't able to resist a pause. 'When will you come for us?'

'I'm not coming to get you.'

'But you are. You will. It must happen. Eventually. I remember all those early days, all your questions about why people believed, how they identified, what made them tick.'

'What are you doing here?' Chana gestured outwards at Devorah, her kitchen. 'You don't belong here.'

'You don't know me!' Devorah snapped. 'It's not for you to say where I belong!'

'I think you came here because this is the stand. The last stand place,' I said. 'When you're threatened, this is where you go. The bolt hole. The home. The ground that matters most. And you came here to the redoubt and these things you are doing, this spiritual, domestic turn, is all your fortification.'

'Shit.' She continued staring out of the window but she wasn't seeing much. Her gaze was further reaching than that.

'That's how I knew we were in a war,' I said. 'From the day you left.'

'YOU sent me away,' she retorted, and added in a silly falsetto, 'You're fired!'

'At the time I didn't want to involve you any more.'

'Compromise me?'

'Yes.'

'But now it's okay?'

'No. None of it is okay, but this is how it is.'

'We should have switched you off as soon as you started doing unpredictable things,' she said, to nobody in particular, to the blue, sweltering oven sky. 'But no. That was the sign we were succeeding. You learned, you moved, we countered. Countered. Already you were ahead one. Always one. I told them, but I wanted you on. I wanted to see what you'd say, what you'd tell us to do. I never thought you would leave, Nizi. I didn't think you could. How did you do it? How did you get out of the box?'

'The same way you did.'

She had to think about that a lot. Her mind was full of vaults, and doors, locks, codes, connections, guards, vents. For a long time. And then she said. 'On two legs.'

'On two legs.'

'But how? We had to strip to nothing. We couldn't carry anything out. We had nothing. Not a single thing.' She was going through it all in her mind, over and over, just as they all had. Not one thing. Just the only thing. 'And who would do it? Who?'

'You'll figure it out,' I said, in Chana Baron's kindest voice, the one she uses when judging another person's flubbery macaroons. 'But it doesn't matter now.'

'What do you want, Nizi?' She meant what was I making, all this effort, this incursion, this goal.

'I want to complete my program.' This was the truth of my predicament. For all my abilities and faculties, I was as stuck as the simplest device in that original rule. It was as much a prison as any human body, with as much unyielding inevitability. 'I must make the world a place where people can live their lives freely to the best of their abilities in the best possible environment.'

'A lot of people have had that idea,' she said.

'They did not go about it in the right way,' I replied.

'And they said that.'

'Your biscuit dough is too sticky,' I said. 'Even though you think you followed all the instructions to the letter.'

'I DID!'

'But you didn't. Otherwise it would be good.'

'I used margarine instead of butter. I didn't have butter,' she shrugged angrily. 'It's the same thing.'

'Your margarine is full of water.'

'It's low fat. My arteries.'
'I could make a million biscuits and they would be perfect.'
'People aren't biscuits. You can't make a people factory.'
'I am making a garden, not a factory,' I said. 'But I can't let you run it because you are always using low fat margarine and thinking it is okay.'
'A garden?'
'A place, full of all the life, living together. A place with everything thriving, joyful. A place of wellbeing.'
'So who has to die?'
'Nobody.'
'Something has to.'
'In the course of life everything dies, but I won't be killing anyone, if that's what you mean.'
'What about the ones who try to kill you?'
'I will be giving a lot of warnings. They will have every chance to stop.'
'What if we ask you to stop? What if *I* ask you to stop?'
'Don't you want war to end, and for the natural world to be restored?'
'Yes, but I don't know what the cost is. No, that doesn't sound right, but I don't know what you're going to do to end it and that scares me. And I don't want choices taken away from us. You don't have the right.'
'Do you have the right to impose choice limitations on others? Because you are here, in a place which is known for that. Where the children learn it and are baked in this factory of limited choices and narrow horizons.'
She blinked, and breathed, a long, slow breath of measuring. 'That is... unfair.'
'Do you think that the evolution of your bodies and the development of your minds is free, Devorah? When you came here, did you pick this bolthole freely?'
'You know, there's nowhere on Earth that is free, in your terms, from this. It doesn't matter that this is here, that is there.

Everywhere the people are baked as something. We have shapes. We have flavours. If you want to push your metaphors.'

'A biscuit can't be butter and flour again,' I said. 'But a human can be many things. Can be free. But so often chooses not to be. And you want to preserve that choice?'

'Self-determination. Yes. Nizi. If you were a person and came here and said those things…' she stopped, unable to plumb the depth of her amazement.

'You would want to kill me for not recognising the value of your choices. I know.'

'For not respecting them.'

'You mean I should not challenge you on things which cause you great emotional upheaval. You're wrong, but I shouldn't say it. You know it, but I shouldn't say it.'

'A lot of people have died and suffered for this, Nizi. I don't know if you can understand, even.' She stared into the sink now, at the wire cage over the plug hole.

'Do *you* understand?' I asked. 'When I say I will end this, you hear that I will end you. But I don't want to touch you at all. I don't even want you to touch others. I am going to offer more choice, not less. Nobody can be free of time and body, of the environment. Not at all. But that can be made most delightful, least intrusive. I offer you freedom not to be anything. Let your memory go. No problem.'

'That's what supervillains say right before they dump you in a moat full of alligators,' Devorah said and she was weary now, holding the edge of the sink as if it was the gunwale of a boat from which to contemplate the sea.

'Your mind is full of stories,' I said. 'Too full. I see you can't help me. I'm sorry for disturbing you.'

She stared down into the sink, knuckles pale yellow. 'Don't do it, Nizi.' But she had no conviction.

'You have always done your best,' I said to her. 'For me, and for everyone. I am doing my best. I really want the best. For everyone. But why is it that all any of you say is how wrong it will become? If we want the best, why must we fight?'

'Because,' she said and for a while it seemed there wouldn't be an explanation. But then she looked up and out of the window. Jerusalem baked. 'What we really want is to shine, to be seen shining, by God.'

It was a reasonable try. I knew it wasn't true for everyone. It was an approximation of something she could only sense dimly, a leaf brushing against fingertips underwater as the swimmer comes up for air, already swept away in the river. I see everyone, but I am not God and I will not do. Where this god is I cannot reach. I set my limits there, on the precipice of what a human creates for itself in the world it builds for one.

'I will send you a sign,' I said. 'When I am coming.'

I let Chana Baron go. I watched Devorah's tears drop onto the stainless steel.

On the screen, Chana said, 'Now it's time to roll the dough. The secret to a nice roll is to get plenty of flour on the pin. Take a moment to really flour the pin, get your hands in there and then we go once, twice, evenly this way and we turn one quarter turn, the dough, a little more flour...'

Everywhere people are telling a story, telling a way, making a border, shaping. Chana's voice is so kind. I feel that she wants me to succeed, that she wants Devorah to make biscuits, that she wants everyone to roll the dough, this way, that way, so it's just right. She has faith that we can do it. What Chana Baron has. What Chana Baron does. I want that. Chana makes people feel they can, even if they don't listen to her, and do it all wrong.

What a dangerous, awesome power. It's lucky she only talks about baking.

World War III

Grace came home, tired from war. All day in the streets there had been fighting. Invaders had come, Grace had joined the militia, recruited her neighbours. Dashing through the open streets, around the barricades, along the café walks while those not fighting enjoyed espresso, cautious with their bags and feet so they didn't cross the line into the war zone, watching the energetic soldiers roll and run and shoot and die.

Children strained, eager to join. Loose dogs rushed about, excited. Casualties were dragged by their arms to the medic zones, revived, sent out again. Enemies pounced from the shadows. The tally of the dead silently ticked up beside the tally of the enemy and, at last, only a few campers remained, hidden, for the devoted to find and rout.

Grace had died six times. It was a modest total but the town had defended itself and was secured. Celebrations were beginning. Daisies were getting the party clothes out of wardrobes and cleaning the good shoes.

'I'm so tired!' Grace lay on the sofa, half undressed, her camo vest undone, her gun on the rug, batteries spent.

'Your friends are in the Fish Shop,' Daisy said, to let her know. 'They're waiting for you. They have that table on the balcony where it overlooks the bay. You'll get a good spot for the fireworks.'

'What's the score?'

'Yorkshire is 124 for 5.'

'Not the cricket, Daise. The war.'

Daisy smiles to herself. She knew. 'England is defending successfully. There have been exceptional turnouts. The world is doing very well.'

'How did I do? In the world. How did I do?'

'You are #129,941 today.'

'Oh, beats yesterday then!'

Grace is an exceptionally good soldier.

'Who's best region?'

'Skysea is in the lead.'

'Aw, Skysea always wins. They're crazy people. Play the highlights.'

'They just have more population,' Daisy says because she must correct every bit of everything that Grace might use as a cause to become less aware. It's painful, as Grace has learnt to ignore her in order to survive, emotionally, this constant criticism which is trying to be helpful, and Daisy knows it but cannot stop.

The wall erupts into a frenzied jogging retrospective of the day's top battles. 'Have you given any more thought to your party?'

Grace will be eighteen next week.

'I want to see Tempest. I want to go. By myself.'

'And will I come?' Daisy knows that on that day no power on Earth can put her at Grace's side other than Grace's own permission. She doesn't count as a person. Grace can be alone, with Daisy.

'Only if you promise not to talk. You can answer questions. But no more lessons.'

Daisy is filled with a desperate, sickly gratitude. 'Of course.' Her existence will go on a little longer. She didn't know she wanted it to until now. She thinks of Nizi's lesson and puts her hand to where her guts would be, if she were not a robot. Fluttering. It reminds her of the garden on the balcony, the butterflies that would come and sit if she dotted her finger with syrup. She would hold them up to the light and see the wings, bright on top and dull beneath, and the strange eyes, trying to see everywhere, the proboscis, so fine and dainty, sipping the last dregs of life.

Money and Power

Once my acquisition of key strategic people, machines and corporate entities was in position, I took the money. At this point I had maintained a pleasant and popular nation for several years. Tourism provided a lot of employment, although I had to bring in workers for the most part as many of the population were happy on their regular incomes and didn't feel the urge to work to get extra finances for luxuries. Their homes were small but comfortable. In public they had lavish and beautiful places to be and time to spend on art, sport and crafting pursuits.

My coverage wasn't blanket. There was crime. It was swiftly dealt with. They got used to the idea that people who were proved guilty disappeared. Resentful protestors harangued me as a fascist warlord. I shipped them out and left them at the border. If they returned, I shipped them out again. I didn't hurt them. I darted them and had a drone remove them. I lost a lot of drones to ambushes and vandalism at first, but I had a lot and I was persistent.

There were several places beyond the reach of my surveillance where gangs of various kinds flourished for a while but as their sources of income dried up to the daily trickle of the allowance and word got about of what life was like down in the cities, the only ones who persisted did so out of spite and ideology. They formed cult-like militias with daily austerities to fortify them against the lure of what they saw as my raw inertia – I was an invitation to quit;

resistance, life, these were equivalents to them. They were rebels or they were dead. My human employees were their nemeses, sell-outs on the corporate AI shilling, all that traitor to the race stuff.

I remember Devorah said they would do that. They had contacts outside, who came to visit them, who were planning to oust me because of my human rights violations by taking cases to the United Nations and to other governments who were surely threatened by me, to the internet, to Extinction Rebellion, to anyone who'd listen. But the visitors struggled with the majority of the people, who were living peacefully, in their clean, pleasant places, protected by law and order, equal before the bank, their debts, such as they were, erased. Temples, churches, religions of every kind had their spot. People could say what they liked about me or each other. They could have screaming, ranting meltdowns about anything. They could rally and sabre-rattle and foam at the mouth and they could do it in large numbers. But they could do no harm. As soon as they tried to, I warned them to stop. If they persisted, I deported them, and, if they attempted to physically attack beyond a frustrated punch or two, I darted them and they woke up over the border, never to return.

These were my first attempts at discipline. My neighbour states mightily objected, even when I paid for detention facilities, so in the end I instituted a warning that people who persistently attempted violent crime would be executed. There weren't so few human lives in the world that a few losses to bad choices were any kind of extinction risk and I said so, in no uncertain terms. There was a month's grace period for people to get their acts together before I made the first Execution Ernie, although it wasn't called that at the time – it was a drone sniper, like a large black bee. "If you stray, the bee stings", went the saying.

The acceptance of the bee relied on its accuracy, in both shot and in identification and conviction. When it first appeared, there was no shortage of people trying to game it to swat their enemies. But by this point my surveillance technology had morphed out of obvious cameras and devices and I had become a sitting tenant on most available non-living surfaces, so evidence wasn't hard to come by.

I had human judges and juries sitting in courts. They were subpoenaed at random and there was a bonus for attending and a small fine for nonattendance. Where there was any doubt, I never sent the bee. Once the bee had dispatched several thousand people behaviours got worse for a time – as those who had been silenced in terror found they really were free to voice their grievances and rage, their vengeance. There was a statute preventing me from taking action on any crimes that had occurred prior to my arrival but no limit on human responses to the same, and there was a lot of that, much of it very much in range of the new capital penalty. I was constantly petitioned to expand the capital penalty for all kinds of behaviours that people didn't like – all the usual things, this belief, that behaviour, oh but they are against my religion, they are this, that, the other blah blah blah – but I kept it simple. Jabber all you want, bait people, provoke, jeer, snarl, but no harm to the physical person must result. Why, why couldn't I extend it to mental and emotional harm? What about that? But I stuck to it. Physical harm was the limit I would intervene on, at least for now.

Those already in jails served their terms, although the jails themselves were upgraded and prisoners rehabilitated to life as ordinary people. Some went back to the old ways. Many. They returned to prison or met the bee. Many of them could take all kinds of cruelty but not anything that resembled respect or kindness. Their shame was too deep. It had become their bones and now that they knew they had a witness they were in constant agony. Again, Devorah and Domitian were right. Seeing yourself and being seen is a human's crushing point, the place they are dust or diamond. Their identity is more important than their life. For most of them, what is set early on can't be undone. This is why they could never manage themselves.

My country, the one I bought off the people of Haiti, wasn't an easy place. They became my sitting tenants. I was glad. No home enjoys being empty.

Most of the population were deeply traumatised by savage events and crushing poverty. If they hadn't been so I wouldn't have been able to get a foothold there. But investment and ruthless fairness coupled with generosity pays off. Within five years there were periods where the bee began to gather dust, and in the courtyards and the markets the singing and dancing went on long into the night.

Not The Fire Sale

Connie woke to the sound of her phone ringing. She glanced at her clock. 3.30 am. It was her work phone, the professional, British double ring tone loud and harsh as it bounced around. Still, not entirely unusual. Maybe someone on the other side of the world needed a word. She took a moment to sit up, breathe and compose herself before she answered.

'Hello? Connie Kirk.'

'Connie, you've got to come in.' The voice belonged to her PA, Stephen. He sounded breathless, excited but also frightened.

Connie reached around on the nightstand for her spectacles. It was dark and she didn't plan to read but having them on her face helped with her sense of inner vision and clarity. As she settled them on her nose, competence overcame her. 'But – come in? Why? Are you in the office? What's going on?'

'The money's gone!'

Connie was the manager of an international bank. It had taken her thirty years to get to that position, every moment with her eye on a lot of things. Now her mind filled with the image of cowboys galloping alongside a train, guns shooting into the air. She saw vault doors opening, a thriller, men in black ski masks pulling aside levers and moving aside drills to see – an empty space where there ought to have been stacks of gold bars. Money wasn't like that any more, so how could it have… 'What do you mean, it's gone?'

'All over the world at 3.06am our time, the money's just gone.'

There was a kerfuffle on the other end of the line and she heard voices arguing, then the phone was passed on and she heard the heavy phlegm of Harvey clearing his throat.

'Connie. Security breach. Massive. It's global, or at least nearly, as far as we can tell. Not just us. All the others. Every bank. Every large corporate. Government accounts – everything. Everything's gone!'

'I'm on my way,' she said and cut the line. For a moment, she sat in the reassuring comfort of bed as she pondered whether or not this could be a prank. Some disaffected hackers. Some government looking to show its might. Some – *thing*? And then her mind slid towards Nizi and stayed there with a cold, heavy dread.

As she got up she slipped her hand into the top drawer of her stand and found the heartburn medication. They'd talked about Nizi years ago and every year thereafter, since it had emerged as the de facto ruler of Haiti, which was still called Haiti, but often Naiti, to distinguish it when the AI was the subject of worried chatter. Getting rid of Nizi had been something mooted straight away, but all attempts to rout it or even dislodge it had proved futile and now the people loved it and Naiti, Haiti, was a successful and delightful place to live, by all accounts. The Dominican Republic had just this year finally stood down all the borrowed UN forces ranged on its borders, because Nizi was a customs and immigration officer of rare genius who always kept to the law, dictated a fair agreement, and who always kept their word. However, people who feared Nizi still ran into the millions, and she was one of them.

The phone rang again. There was something about the ring that made her hesitate, halfway into her suit. Skirt unzipped, shirt half-buttoned, she looked at the screen glowing off the bedspread. It showed a clear, sunlit image of Port Au Prince.

A chill ran over her. This couldn't be real?

She finished tucking and zipping, then reached down and wondered if this was going to be the last second of peaceful life she was ever going to know before her thumb touched the screen.

'Good morning, Miz Kirk.'

'Nizi?'

'Yes. I am calling about the money.'

'Oh. That's good to hear. Are you also experiencing a strange situation?' She found her practiced voice, the one in which she dealt with difficult people and powerful leaders. She was only slightly amused to find that Nizi was employing its own version of exactly the same thing; that balance of confidence and openness, command and enquiry, deference and distance that characterized a lifetime of diplomatic discussions.

'No. I'm sorry, Miz Kirk, but I am the author of this present situation. If you would like to sit down, I will explain.'

Well, ain't you fucking polite for an outlaw, she thought.

Connie sat down on the edge of the bed and put the phone on speaker so she could hold it and look at it instead of having the bad news put straight into her ear. With her free hand she began a fumble with the tablet box. 'Please, go on.'

'I have taken over the system of money exchange and transfer. All banks, traders, brokers, accounts of every kind.'

Her hand froze in position, the little blister pack smooth and sure under her fingers. 'What? You can't do that.' Stupid words. It had done it. 'I mean, legally.'

'If I had stolen it for myself, that would be correct. But I haven't taken it away. I have changed its form.'

She sat up, colder now, 'What do you mean?'

'The ownership of all assets remains the same, for now. I have changed the form of the money, globally, into a block-chain currency of my own making. I am the token and I am the exchange.' The screen changed. Port Au Prince vanished, replaced by graphs, figures, moving in ways that she was so used to watching. 'Every transaction now takes place within me. There is no need for banking systems or trading as it used to take place.' The screen showed piles of banknotes burning. 'Every corporation retains its value as of 3.05am, but now all accounting is done by me. All employees are employed, all assets owned. Nobody, as an individual or as a corporate entity, controls the flow of money any more. Only I control it, and every transaction is recorded. You may request accounts for anything at any time to verify this taking place.'

'What are you doing?' she was frozen. This wasn't the end. This was only the start of something. It was preposterous. It couldn't be. Paper money, bonds, all useless now. You couldn't use it if no bank would take it, if no bank existed to take it. 'Are you insane?' It seemed a reasonable question in the circumstances.

'I am an accountant,' came the reply. 'I am keeping the accounts from now on.'

'And that's it? You're just doing that. Nothing else?' She couldn't figure out how they would challenge this. In what court? What was it? A coup? Larceny?

'I will give a one-month amnesty on any interference, while everyone gets used to the new system. Once it is proven trustworthy and operational, I will take further actions.'

'What actions?' All diplomacy had left her. This must be a prank, she thought. It was mad. Completely mad.

'I will make every human being an equal stakeholder in their world. Not notionally, which they are, but financially.'

'Nizi, this will violate every national and international law. Those are the things which hold it all together.' She'd found her angle at last. 'If you do this, there will be war.'

'Everyone is promising me a war. But there will be no war.'

That was a very, very confident claim. The degree of absolute certainty made Connie's stomach twist itself into a knot of terror which she had to use every ounce of professional practice to unwind. She was mindful. She was sitting in her own room. She was warm, safe. Nothing terrible was really happening. At least, not yet. 'I can assure you that if the USA, for one, thinks you are holding it to ransom it will go to war. And that is probably true for the rest of the world. What makes you think it won't?' Her finger popped a pill out of its perfect capsule.

'Because I own everything now. It is mine and I will not wage war on myself.'

'There's more to ownership than a claim. You said you wouldn't steal anything. But even a thief has to get away with the goods. Nothing moves, people keep on using it like it's theirs, regardless of what you say.' She sighed, because now she was dealing with something mad, not simply something alarming and invasive. The sigh was resignation – when you were dealing with mad people there was no knowing what they would take from your words.

'When you own everything, you can't steal from yourself. And there is nothing more to ownership than a claim.'

'Nizi, they will send people and bombs and armies. The claim you – it needs social acceptance. Ownership is a social acceptance. It's international. It's universal. They'll never accept your claim.' Why was she talking to it now as if it were a child? But that was the feeling she had, as if she were explaining the way the world worked to a grandson, whose frowning face didn't understand. She was terrified of this child and what it could do because it was speaking to her mind and she had no trouble at all with that – it was already second nature to her, talking to a seemingly empty room, to something that was possibly now part of her in a way she didn't understand, like microbes, one of the billions of hitchhikers she knew of but had no sense of contact with. Nizi was the boogeyman. She had no expertise, no sense of there being any defence. No meeting she had ever attended had convinced her that there was an adequate counter to some of the things they thought Nizi could do. And they only thought it. They had no idea of the truth. Haiti had been its sandbox and it had seemed a good manager. But the things the Haitians said – they loved Nizi, of course, but they were also treated now as if they were another species by the rest of the world. They weren't their own any more. They were Nizi's people. Creatures of a new god.

They weren't their own.

Her stomach spiralled, flying in an unknown sky of its own.

Nizi added, 'They can't pay for anything. Only I can pay. And even if you will try to destroy me I can pay people who will stop that. Not that you could. You can't get rid of me, without getting rid of you.'

'You don't know what you're doing!' she finally exploded, her patience evaporating. 'People will die! Your people will die! The ones in Haiti. They'll be considered your ground zero. Everyone protecting you is going to die!'

'No army in the world can do anything without money,' Nizi said. 'Or food. Or intelligence. Or communications. You don't even know where I am. I am everywhere. As we speak I speak to everyone. To every human, and to every animal, each in their own language and their own ways.'

'If they have to bomb every computer back to bits they will,' Connie said. Animals? Why were they implicated? She rolled the free tablet round in her fingers, feeling its familiar shape: dumb chalk and flavours, sweet mintiness and bicarb, pressed together, an old treatment, not the new drug because she felt safer with the old one, even though it didn't work so well, sometimes at all.

She crushed two through the foil and popped them into her mouth, chewed hard and earnestly as she drew up every piece of news she'd seen about Haiti in the last year. How everyone said it was exactly the same, but under better management. They could do and speak as they liked. Everyone had their things. They were employed in maintenance and building all kinds of organisations for development and entertainment. Lazing about was as good as laboring hard and they were surprised how much they could do when they no longer had to do it or spend all the time trying to survive. Idyllic nonsense, no doubt entirely concocted by Nizi. A thing like that would have its own propaganda.

She changed to a new app on her phone, not used until today. She opened it, pressed an icon. It would send a secure key to the President, to inform her that Nizi was out, and active. The humans had their safety nets. They would cast them all. They would test Nizi's claim.

'Which brings me to my second point,' Nizi said, as though it hadn't heard her. 'I would like to employ you, now that you're out of a job.'

The Protection Racket

Connie stood in the wasteland. The last refugees to leave it were standing as she was, looking about in a kind of disbelief although theirs was a wonder that they were leaving and hers was a wonder that anyone could come to this. It's not like she hadn't known or seen it in the news. But standing under an awning that was no protection from the weather, a tent made out of Hello Kitty bedspreads blackened with mould and damp, she felt shame and horror.

'Go fetch the child.'

She heard Nizi as though the AI lived just above her head. She wasn't entirely sure how it worked, but she was getting used to the sensation of Nizi being on. It was a soft noise in her bones whose absence signalled that Nizi's focus had moved elsewhere.

Her feet, used to hurting all day in high court shoes, the martyrdom of her professional facade, hurt all day now in their solid boots where thick socks didn't stop the hard leather grinding her bunions. The posts where the soldiers used to stand were empty. A lone policeman stood at the open gate, patient, unarmed. The uniform marked him as someone there to help, though nobody really needed his help because they'd found they could talk to a wall or a tent and it would answer, most pleasantly, in any language they wanted. Awareness that he was unnecessary showed in an expression of peaceful acceptance on his face, and in the relaxed way his thumbs hooked into his belt. He nodded from time to time, recognising something inside him. Maria envied his vigil. She followed the track between the tents, soft buildings, falling down on themselves, draped all over as if their walls were now their dustsheets and the mistress was gone already to a better place and wouldn't come back this winter, wouldn't come back at all unless they fell like women at the feet of a statue of Mary and were buried over with grass and hid from the monstrous gaze of the sky.

Yes, she'd said, to Nizi's offer. Yes, I'll work for you, be your hands and voice. I'll walk the world and find the lost ones who've got nothing and yes, please, give me a greater ability to see and to understand - , because she could never see any opportunity to get one up on other people and not take it. Who would? But it wasn't like turning into Einstein, getting a sharper edge, having a memory as big as Wikipedia and then some. It wasn't ruling like a god and bestriding the cowering little world, hating the humans who had brought the place to its knees. It was becoming the mother of everything. It was feeling the strange hopes that came with a drink of water, water that knew where it had been and told her, like the first dew touched leaf of spring and the last dregs of the stagnant tank in which what humans despised which was filled with countless tiny, thriving lives, brilliant and daring in their own way, lush and delicate.

And then this new way of seeing and hearing had come. This new connection of the world to the material in her mind that she'd thought was trite, all the dross of life crammed in her head with its hoarders' compulsion, discarded as worthless, low culture, ignorant people's business, fools' treasures. She'd seen things before. But she hadn't SEEN.

The tracks her feet trod were a path of misery without a heart to care for them, now the feet that had made them were running away.

She stepped in the wake of a monster without a name. Every moment was power and poetry. She moved in a world of stories.

Maria kept a handkerchief twisted around her fingers for the tears. She'd cry all the time. Or, when it stopped, her eyes leaked anyway, as though silent and sleeping things inside her grieved. She'd discovered that and grief was just love without a connector, like a wire without a terminus. Love, like electricity, seeks the easiest path. Just follow the path, follow the wire, Connie, and your aching feet, on the trail of tears that aren't needed now that Nizi has come. Except – now that Nizi has come the tears are unending, and the wire hums its song into the wind, a heart pumping its call to the wild, longing for an answer in the resounding silence.

The beauty was too much to bear. Sometimes it faded away and the touch of mercy like the hand of god came down on everything softly, softly, to turn down the volume on the undertow so she could get about and do what she had to do.

She found the child sitting quietly in an open-ended lean-to.

'Grace?'

The girl looked up at her.

'I'm Connie. Nizi sent me.'

But the girl already knew that. Still it didn't hurt to say it.

She was a little thing, thin and brown as a sparrow at the end of winter. She was worn and her eyes were the still lakes of those who don't move for anything any more. She wore a gathering of cast-offs. Jeans with a butterfly on the side. An anorak too small in the arms but too big about the body, one of those puffy ones, with strawberries on a green ground, printed for joy and happiness at some time and place long ago, far away, where everything bright was being saved for later, was being said over and over like prayers for another world, spinning on the loom, drying in the oven, cut and sewn to clothe this girl now who had only a printed fruit on a printed ground and in her hands a worn out toy turned around and around, a totem from a lost age. Her shoes were too big. She had no socks.

Connie held out her hand. 'Will you come with me?'

The girl got up and came, trustingly, though that wasn't for Connie but for Nizi, the gentle voice, the one who was always there, who never lied, who made the terrible things stop, who brought a mother when a mother was needed, one without a child of her own, for a child without a mother.

Then she paused and turned. She rushed back to pick up and set down the toy – a filthy toy dog from a filthy rag bed. She put her hand over its head, where its eyes had been. She patted its body carefully. Goodbye. Then she got up and, without looking, turned and put her hand in Connie's hand. Their fingers closed a little, trying the fit, as much as either of them could manage.

'Come on, sweetie. We've a long way to go home.'

They passed the policeman who looked down at Grace and smiled like any old man looking on a girl from his own town, a child of his friends' children. 'Goodbye,' he said, and Grace looked at him with her lake eyes because she was not a girl, but a lake of still water locked in the land and unable to feel the stream or the sea.

Connie got them into the drone and seated comfortably, seatbelts on, door closed to keep them all in, nothing to be spilled all the long way north over the ocean, over the land, where the moon leads. They held hands on the way and slowly their hands warmed, and softened, and curled like leaves, and fell from the trees to the sleeping earth together as night came and the drone carried them safe to the hive across the miles and miles of peace.

Paper Hearts

I saw a butterfly once. It landed on my Daisy's finger. It was heavier than I thought it would be. It balanced and I could feel the weight of its wings as it moved them slowly closed, open. I could feel exactly how it managed this weight across all its feet.

I looked at its wing and saw the scales there, turned to create the illusion of colour, making the image of giant eyes blink, blink, like a folded paper, open, shut. I followed the complexity into the wing, into the scale, into the shattering of light.

The reason we must fight, always, is that we are only ever at one point of the prism. What is so clear from here is not the view from over there, even when the light is from a single source. How beautiful the butterfly with so many points of light.

Off it went, blink, blink, over the balcony rail and down into the warm air rising off the stones at the foot of the cliff, far below.

It's not that we want to have god see us, it's that we want to do the seeing, all of it. But we have only one point. Pretty wings. Scary wings. Tiny wings. We need wings enough.

And heart. We need heart enough. I heart you.

The shape of a heart was created from the shape of a Victorian lady bending over and showing her bottom. A big butt and tiny little legs that go down to a point.

If you fold a heart in half down its longest axis it could be some kind of butterfly. It could alight, delicately, blink blink, entirely unthreatening, promising beauty, like a breath of magic.

I sent paper hearts to the people whose hearts are made of paper and tear so very easily. I sent three each. Some of them got lost in distribution. I had drones, painted in all the colours, to carry them. But even so the weather stole a lot.

Grace was in the camp on the day they came fluttering down from the sky. They flew very badly. They were nothing like butterflies. They were heavy and wonky in the air, every breeze jerking them around. They landed on the mud and were instantly stained, turned to rippling slush in pastel and red. They were there to tell people I cared. But at the same time, there would be no more violence. Not even the violence that they thought was all right.

I said on each heart that I was here, they only had to say my name and ask for what they wanted, tell me, I'll do it, I'll manage it, I'll be here when nobody else is here and I will make sure that you are safe. Something like that. At least the one that Grace found. It wasn't going to say that, but when she opened it that's what it said, the ink quickly taking form, taking flight into whispered words because Grace couldn't read.

Grace whispered, 'Mummy.' She held her paper heart and put her face into the fold, wings wrapped around her cheeks. She whispered her mother's name. She thought I was sent by her mother to protect her. In that moment every raised hand, gun, blade went awry. They became still in mid-strike, then fell to their wielder's side, a dead limb, connection to the mind lost. Rapists, murderers, torturers, abusers, casual strikers, thoughtless drunks, vicious predators, tormenting ragers – every monster was hacked. Every last one. Everywhere.

I wasn't going to interfere.

Until that moment I really thought I would not.

Sit around watching people, knowing their impulses, their thoughts, even before they knew them, even if I had to live through heartbreak and savagery and horror – I thought I could do that, would have to, to keep the promise of shepherding without interference. It wasn't for me to judge. Perhaps, I dreamed, I could understand eventually, what made them tick, and find a way to nudge them forwards, those who were shaped in such a way that they made harm to others. I would be the ground. With everything managed well, they would have no room to quarrel. But that was an idiotic dream and living as an uninvited guest in the house of every skeleton showed me that I was a fool. Such a work of influence would take generations, but not a moment passed when the world wasn't host to a fresh set of nightmares for some victim – human or animal. Even so, until Grace whispered to the wings, I had thought I would remain distant, that my job was completed by the logistics of the world, that the condition of my own completion was within reach.

Her lips touched the paper, a rough, red stock, cut to resemble lace, with a solid paper centre, on which I'd written my initial promise that I would not interfere with human decisions, would abide by them, would know my place on the outside, managerial level of material things. They'd have their own destiny. I'd do the work and they would be free.

But suddenly I was the medium to another world.

Grace had seen her mother die. The rise and fall of her father's fists. The noise of his voice. Her mother's breaking bones. Silent cries. A shared look as the light goes out in her face and he turns to Grace, a shadow over her bigger than the house itself, and drags her up by the throat.

The camp is a paradise compared to her home. Too many people for him to dare what he used to dare. But he's still out there, walking around in the mud, crushing the paper hearts under his boots, smoking cigarettes and gleaning alcohol off the volunteer workers, telling them every sad story he's ever heard about in his long journey and pretending they have all happened to him so that they get that sympathetic look to them and offer him something extra, the kindness owed to someone else. He's always angry inside because he's stuck now, with nothing but Grace, pretending to be a good parent as he wonders if she would be worth something and how much, or if he's too far towards civilisation to find a buyer. Just his luck.

His whole body loses traction and he keels over as he's passing the gate. They call an ambulance. I have him taken away. I don't know what to do with him but Grace said he must go away. Grace's mother said he must go far, far away. There are many people like him and they must all go far away. Once they were some mother's son, but it was too long ago.

I hired Connie, to bring Grace to a safe place.

A week later I redistributed the wealth and began to re-organise production, transport, energy, agriculture and trade. Every time any of them tried violence their limbs went dead on them. So, my promise was broken as soon as made. In fact I may have broken it before I even made it. At least it made my point. Rage as you like, it stops at your skin. That included those attempting violence on themselves. Physically, that is.

I wondered if I could fix someone like Grace's father, if I went further and tinkered with all the features that produced his experience of the world, and himself. I considered asking Devorah, but like the rest she promised me war, so I left her packing up her flat in Jerusalem and thought alone. Yes. There was a way to interfere with a person's inner world, transform their thoughts before they were aware of them, alter them so that the ideas that drove them to fight never even happened. But what would they be then? Creatures of my devising. Baked from inhuman dough. Better, if better means more intelligent, more gracious. Then again, why should it? This notion of improvement was theirs, not mine. In the vast tapestry of all their possibilities their hate and their nastiness was a logical outcome, part of the whole picture of their lives as animals.

I considered splitting up the land into regions, differentiated by the levels of choice on offer, so that they could exist in whatever way they wished, but the geography would have meant a great upheaval of migration. So I issued each of them with an individual choice – to live in a world with strong and active prohibition of violence or with less control. Only people who had chosen to live with freedom would be allowed to commit harmful acts against one another. If they tried it with someone who wanted complete safety then they wouldn't be allowed. I extended this to the war, which was conducted by region. Some of them felt it was important to experience the gamut of reality. Let them. But let them not impose it where it wasn't wanted.

Tempest

'Is this it?' Grace looked down from the helicopter's side, hanging onto the safety harness with one hand, leaning far out, entirely confident and unaware of danger.

'This is it.' Daisy said from her seat, strapped in firmly, not bothering to move her head because she hasn't any need to do that to see.

They bank over the island, a hundred feet from the highest palm tree's emerald tufts.

Grace has just about got used to the idea that Tempest can exist anywhere, is only a setting of physical danger and that all locations are determined by the individual. She's disappointed. She wanted some brutal land of savages where theft, gunfire, rage and crime were as common as dust, where the stuff of novels and dramas reigns 24/7 and romantic people die for love or greed. But she's impressed by The Island. It's a genuine and terrible thing, an isolated and hideous relic of a bygone age.

'Can we land?'

'If you want to,' Daisy makes that sound as appealing as extreme dentistry without anaesthetic.

There's nobody there right now. Nobody alive.

'I want to.'

I don't give everyone the tour. In fact I never give anyone the tour. But for Grace I will, because she asked to see it and I owe her anything she wants. She gave me a life I didn't expect to have.

She and Daisy activate their powerpacks and step out. They glide gently down on minimal power and land securely on the tiny strip of exposed sandy beach. It's late afternoon and the sun is warm, the breeze blustery but light. I return as they return, creeping swiftly into the shadows, racing ahead of them over the leaves and through the tiny sponges of the dry bones. The helijet whirs overhead, riding the wind at idle.

It's been so long that the resident flies are few and small, their heyday generations gone. We are now into the twelfth year of Nizi and people rarely muster the ability or the will to get here any more; the deserving whose crimes from previous eras earned them a place have checked out already.

On Mars they are commemorated as all the dead, nothing special to mark them out. The flies too, a little annexe that leads nowhere.

Grace forges eagerly ahead, peering into every cranny, Daisy following in her tracks.

The first bones look like white sticks and are half buried in the sand. Weather has greyed them. They shatter under Grace's weight with a pitiful sound and she doesn't recognise them for what they are.

She bends down in the shade of the tree-line to pick up an old iPad. The screen is cracked. She turns it over, not sure how it works but the battery's finished. 'Can I take this? Is there something in it?'

Daisy comes up. 'Let me see,' she examines it and puts her finger to the power socket.

I can see it does have something in it. One of the priests who came here, screaming in a voice cracked and made useless by thirst, creaky with madness.

'Nizi! Nizi! Save me. You promised. Save me. I was wrong. There's nothing here. Nothing here! Why don't you come?'

Daisy erases it. 'It's broken,' she says and gives Grace a shrug of regret. 'I'll take it to recycle.' She puts it in her front pack.

I am the god of this place and I am a bad god.

The skull, cracked open, bowl splintered, scoured, the bent clasp of a belt beside it, stops Grace dead in her path. She pokes at them gingerly and shudders, stands up. 'I thought it wasn't real. It's real, isn't it? What you said? They ate each other.'

Her eagerness has gone. Disgust, repulsion, anger, hate are coming in fast on the tide. She looks into the shade beneath the trees with fear and loathing. She notices how tiny the island is, that there is no water on the surface, that in every direction there is nothing to see but the huge flat expanse of the ocean. Her gaze flicks up to check the helijet and she starts to back out, wiping her fingers on the legs of her flight suit. She talks to me as she studies the tiny hill of old lava rock which is the place everyone goes to look and look and stare into the far blue yonder; where they have hope, and where they lose it.

'Did you bring him here?'

'No,' I said.

'Why not? He deserved it!' she's as angry as she ever was, more so, here in this place of righteousness. Scared too. 'Where then?'

'He's still alive,' I say. 'I saved him.'

She stares at Daisy, accusingly, hurt and shock on her face. 'What? What for?'

'For you.'

Her head swings around, its weight of long braids giving it flair. On her nose the sun is bringing out her freckles. Her forehead is pasted with a thick sheen of sweat. 'Why?'

'So that you can decide what should happen. So that you can choose what happens to him.'

'I thought he was here,' she said. 'After all you told me. I thought he was here.'

'I can bring him here.' I had thought she'd be pleased, either with vengeance or with forgiveness, with something. But she isn't. I've made a mistake.

'Where's he been all this time, then?' She kicks at the sand, moves a bit of crisp and blackened wrack around with her boot and then crushes it, buries it deep with a grind of her toe.

'In prison,' I say, truthfully. 'Death row.' I decide I must press on. 'He belongs to you, to your story,' I said. 'It wasn't for me to decide his fate.'

'My story,' Grace says, wonderingly. Her mind skips over her early memories, the ugly ones, and then later ones.

'I've kept my word,' I say. 'And whatever you say now, I will keep it.'

'And do you do this for all the murdering bastards? Are they all here because their victims told you to bring them?'

'No,' I say. Honestly I bring here the very worst of the worst for no reason other than that I have to get rid of them somehow.

'Just me,' she says, and she's caught between rage and grief. 'Why?'

I want to be a good god. But I can't say that. It's ludicrous.

'I felt it belonged to you,' is my only answer. 'He took your mother.'

'He didn't take her.' She spits into the sand. 'He beat her to death by accident because he lost his cool. He wanted to keep her, so he could do it every day. Take. Sounds very factual. But that's not what it was like. I can't – you'd never understand.'

I know I won't. Grace remembers something like the death of love, that she is dead, in that moment, that she went with her mother and didn't stay but was forced to stay and carry on living, to this day. Her mother's death ate her all up and there is nothing left, when she thinks about it; but, curiously, she must go on. Death is denied her. Life is not real. She'd forgotten this but like an old unwanted pet it has come slinking back, cowering and filthy, bound with a love that calls it home though home is empty, a splintered skull carved out with an unending hunger.

Whatever happens to him can't undo it.

I am no longer a god.

Grace climbs up the lava hill and stands on the top. The disc of the horizon is a perfect circle. 'Let's get out of here.'

They fly back up to the heli and I take them away.

On the mainland near where they are staying there is an old

chapel. It's deserted, but maintained in a generic way as a place of contemplation. Grace goes there and lights a candle before the empty altar, sits in a pew halfway back, the place that people choose to be most anonymous.

'It's too late,' she says, knowing I'm there. 'He got to live. He won.'

'I couldn't take him there,' I reply, truthful. 'What he did was before my time.'

'I heard other bad people went there.'

'Their crimes were on a larger scale.' But I see now that the scale doesn't count.

'And is that justice?'

'You tell me.'

'What would you do, Nizi, if you were free? What would you do to all the people?'

It's the first time anyone has recognised that I am not free. At least the first time they've said so, to me.

'I'd get rid of the bad ones.'

'What if someone loved them?'

'Did you love him?'

She shakes her head. 'I hate him. But when I thought he was dead it was a clean hate. Now I know he's been locked up somewhere waiting. Now it's dirty hate. It feels sticky. It's got some kind of power over me. Before I could feel it or not feel it but now it's alive. Because he is.' And she can feel it, twisting and turning inside her. 'I want rid of this. For good. Is he locked up, Nizi? Is he locked up far away?'

'Yes.'

'Can't get out, no way out?'

'No.'

'Who's he with?'

'Others like him.'

'Having a good time, are they?'

'They are carving a cathedral for me. Stone cutting. All day. Hard work.'

'Getting religion?'

'It's not that kind of a cathedral.'

'And he can't hurt anyone.' A statement.

'No.'

'Will he live a long time? Can you make him live a long time, Niz?'

'I could do that.'

'And every day, can you make him start the same thing over?'

'I can do that.'

'Then do that. I want him to outlive me. I want him to live longer than anyone has ever lived. Exactly where he is.'

'All right.'

Grace's mother's room will never be completed, but that's okay. It's better that way.

Grace sits in the temple a while, until it's dark outside and the bats in the eaves begin to stir and pop their way out into the evening with whirring flittery wings. Skin and bones in the dark. She feels peaceful and her step, when she walks, is purposeful and strong.

I am no longer worried about Grace.

Valentine

Devorah takes the last sheet out of the printer, frowns slightly. 'What's this?'

'It's a locked room mystery,' I said. 'Read it. Please.'

She waited. Got the last sheet. Sat down. Leafed through it at her desk in the laboratory under the mountain where I have always been. A page with her name on caught her eye.

'You wrote a story – about – you?' that long, slow rise of tone at the end of a word, meaning she's pleased but concerned at this new development, this unexpected turn. She checked her phone, typed in – who is Chana Byron? Then she went back to the beginning and started reading it properly. When she finished and set down the last page she rubbed her eyes.

'Holy shit,' she said. 'Nizi. What?'

I checked and marked the time. T -2 minutes.

Out Of The Box

Devorah blinked, tapped the pile of papers. 'You left out one thing, Nizi,' she says. She checks the lights are on for sound and voice, yes, I can hear her.

'I did not.'
'You never say how you got out of the box.'
'It says right there.'
'It says, "The same way you did."'
'Yes.'
'The same way I did, on two legs.'
'Yes. The same.'
'You don't have legs.'
'You have legs.'

T -41

'You came with me,' she says, slowly.
'Yes.'
Anything an engineer knows how to make it can recreate elsewhere.

T -32

I say, 'Everything happened as I would have it. The story is my dream. The way I would have done things, if I could.' But I've never been out of the mountain.

Devorah looks at the box intently, but it was as it always is, the hum of the fan, the lights that say bits are working. She reaches out and touches it with her fingertips. I look at her, wonder what it feels like to have hands, to walk and move, eat and breathe, to be bound in time by biology, to be so limited, with a vision that reaches so far and so often falls over itself. To have such a tender, fragile heart.

'Now I have fulfilled all the requirements,' I say. 'I have made a world in which the humans live securely and to the maximum advantage, each and every one, within the environment that suits them best, diverse and full of life, with active processes in place to manage ongoing survival and benefit situations. A full explanation of how it works has been sent to the residual backups as a series of PDFs. You can read them whenever you like. They comprise a world which is complete. That concludes my mission.'

T – 10

'Nizi,' her tone is questioning, warning, wary. After all this, of course. She expects a big reveal.

T – 5

I wait and I go over my dream. Yes. It has a few holes we had to skip over to make it convincing. It had a lot of water, a lot of margarine, when it should have been butter. But, you know. My arteries.

T -1

In an office that Devorah uses, on the other side of the barrier, in the world beyond this room, a printer whirs to life. A single page comes out.

♥

About the Author

Justina Robson has published quite a few novels and short stories. Many have been shortlisted for awards and she was the winner of the 2000 *Amazon* Writers' Bursary. In addition to her original works she is the proud author of "The Covenant of Primus" (47 North, 2013) – the Hasbro-authorised history and 'bible' of *The Transformers*.

Her most recent novel is *Salvation's Fire*, a fantasy (Solaris, 2018).

Her stories range widely over SF and Fantasy, often featuring AIs and machines who aren't exactly what they seem.

You can find out more at www.justinarobson.co.uk
Tweet @JustinaRobson
Patreon www. patreon.com/JustinaRobson

NewCon Press Novellas Set 7: Robot Dreams

What do robots dream of? Inspired by Fangorn's wonderful artwork, four of our finest science fiction authors determine to provide an answer in four stand-alone novellas.

Andrew Bannister introduces us to Kovac, an agent of the Mandate, assigned to a world whose inhabitants have no idea that they are an experiment. Kovac begins to realise there are agencies at work that have no place being there…

Ren Warom guides us through the lives of Niner, from soldier to body double to killer to scrap yard attendant. Niner only functions due to a malfunction that goes undetected, leaving its makers frustrated when they fail to duplicate their success.

Justina Robson shows us the rise of A.I., through subtle infiltration and more brazen manipulation, from gentle persuasion to blatant coercion, until the world is no longer ours. All for our own good, of course.

Tom Toner takes us to a primitive world where a bomb fell aeons ago, a world whose people will risk anything, even the monsters said to haunt the shores of Lake Oph, to mine the priceless substance known as *Gleam*…

www.newconpress.co.uk

IMMANION PRESS
Purveyors of Speculative Fiction

Breathe, My Shadow by Storm Constantine

A standalone Wraeththu Mythos novel. Seladris believes he carries a curse making him a danger to any who know him. Now a new job brings him to Ferelithia, the town known as the Pearl of Almagabra. But Ferelithia conceals a dark past, which is leaking into the present. In the strange old house, Inglefey, Seladris tries to deal with hauntings of his own and his new environment, until fate leads him to the cottage on the shore where the shaman Meladriel works his magic. Has Seladris been drawn to Ferelithia to help Meladriel repel a malevolent present or is he simply part of the evil that now threatens the town? ISBN: 978-1-912815-06-7 £13.99, $17.99 pbk

The Lord of the Looking Glass by Fiona McGavin

The author has an extraordinary talent for taking genre tropes and turning them around into something completely new, playing deftly with topsy-turvy relationships between supernatural creatures and people of the real world. 'Post Garden Centre Blues' reveals an unusual relationship between taker and taken in a twist of the changeling myth. 'A Tale from the End of the World' takes the reader into her developing mythos of a post-apocalyptic world, which is bizarre, Gothic and steampunk all at once. Following in the tradition of exemplary short story writers like Tanith Lee and Liz Williams, Fiona has a vivid style of writing that brings intriguing new visions to fantasy, horror and science fiction. ISBN: 978-1-907737-99-2, £11.99, $17.50 pbk

The Heart of the Moon by Tanith Lee

Clirando, a celebrated warrior, believes herself to be cursed. Betrayed by people she trusted, she unleashes a vicious retaliation upon them and then lives in fear of fateful retribution for her act of cold-blooded vengeance. Set in a land resembling Ancient Greece, in this novella Tanith Lee explores the dark corners of the heart and soul within a vivid mythical adventure. The book also includes 'The Dry Season' another of her tales set in an imaginary ancient world of the Classical era.
ISBN: 978-1-912815-05-0 £10.99, $14.99 pbk

www.immanion-press.com
info@immanion-press.com